AMISH WIDOW'S CHRISTMAS

EXPECTANT AMISH WIDOWS BOOK 12

SAMANTHA PRICE

D1519192

AMISH ROMANCE

CHAPTER 1

The Lord is my light and my salvation; whom
shall I fear?
the Lord is the strength of my life;
of whom shall I be afraid?
Psalm 27:1

SARAH LOOKED up in fright as Matilda breezed through the door waving an envelope.

"What's that?" Sarah asked, her eyes fixed on the moving object.

"A letter. I met the postman just as he pulled up to put it in the box. I wonder who it could be from. Perhaps it's from some distant relative asking you to come visit them. Or maybe it's a childhood friend you haven't seen in years."

"I don't think so." Sighing, Sarah shook her head. "It would be nice to get a letter once in awhile. It's another bill; that's what it is."

Matilda sat on the couch next to Sarah. She looked at the envelope and flipped it over. "Looks like a letter to me," Matilda said. "And such nice handwriting."

"Trust me, it's another bill." Sarah shook her head again. "I can't open it. I just can't. I can't face another bill."

"Whatever it is, I'm sure it can wait for another day." Matilda leaned over and placed it on the coffee table and leaned back. "How are you feeling today anyway? Still bored and cranky?"

Sarah sighed. "Yeah, about the same. I just want my *boppli* in my arms and then I'll feel better. We can face the world together. Then the bills won't matter so much."

"I know things are hard right now, but that doesn't mean things will be that way forever. Tom and I went through some hard times, and then things changed for us. He was out of work for about six months. At the time, it seemed like it would last forever."

Sarah smiled at her friend who was like a sister to her. If Matilda were in this position, Sarah knew that she'd be saying exactly the same kind of things to her. "I just don't know what I'm going to do. I've got enough money for maybe another two months and then what do I do?" She laid a hand on her swollen belly. She was about to give birth any day.

"Please stay with Tom and me until you

get on your feet. You can stay as long as you want."

Matilda had asked her many a time and Sarah had always refused, but now it was looking like the only option. *"Denke.* That's a kind offer, but you know how I hate to impose."

Matilda was a good friend, but it was times like these when Sarah wished she had family. She'd been an only child born to older parents who had since gone home to God, and then her husband had died five months ago. They'd been married since she was eighteen and he had been her whole world.

"You'll look back on this time a year from now and you'll be amazed how much your life has changed for the better. *Gott* will provide for you. I know it. I've never been more sure about anything in my life. He will provide."

As much as Sarah wanted to believe her friend, she couldn't. So many things had gone wrong, starting when Joel had died, that it was hard to believe that things would ever get better.

"I hope you're right about that."

"You shouldn't have to worry about anything now. You should be enjoying the last days of your pregnancy."

"I do feel a little better now that I know I can stay at your place. Are you sure Tom won't mind?"

"We've talked about it and he wants you to stay."

Matilda and Tom had four children, and that was another reason Sarah had resisted taking up her offer. She didn't want to be in the way and she also didn't want to take charity; she wanted to be in a position to provide for herself and her child.

"When did you last eat?" Matilda asked.

"I can't eat too much at the moment because this baby is squashing my stomach and taking up all the room."

Matilda giggled. "What have you got for the evening meal?"

"Don't fuss, Matilda, you're my friend not my *mudder*."

"I have to watch over you."

"And I'm sorry that the burden has fallen on you."

"It's not a burden, Sarah. You're like a *schweschder* to me. I've already figured I can put my *kinner* in the same room and you can have the bedroom overlooking the pond. Alright?"

Sarah nodded. *"Denke.* As long as it's truly alright with Tom."

"He wants to have you there, and he loves babies. When do you have to be out of here?"

"In four weeks. I just gave my notice to Mrs. Collins yesterday and told her I'd be out at the end of the month."

"Don't worry about anything. We'll store your furniture in the barn and I'll organize the ladies to help you pack. Tom can get a few men together and he'll borrow his *bruder's* long wagon to load everything."

Holding her head, Sarah found it hard to comprehend all of the things that would happen after the birth of her child. The main thing she wanted to concentrate on was her baby's safe arrival into the world. Her stomach churned with the anxiety of the unknown. The worst thing would be if she went to Matilda's house and felt that she was in their way. What if she never got any money to enable her to leave their house—what then?

"Now, have you got everything ready for the *boppli?*"

Noticing Matilda's gaze had come to rest on a pile of sewing on a chair, Sarah said, "That lot's been done and is ready for them to collect it tomorrow."

Since Joel had lost his job due to cutbacks, Sarah had taken in alterations for the local tailor. The work she got from them put food on the table but wasn't enough to cover the rent. Her last money had gone on Joel's funeral expenses and the last month's rent. Now, she had to face living on the kindness of the community.

"I should go. My *kinner* will be home from *schul* anytime now."

"*Denke* for stopping by, Matilda. I don't know what I'd be like if it weren't for you these past few months."

"I'll stop by again tomorrow and I hope you'll be able to tell me that you've had some signs of your *boppli* coming."

"Florence says that I might have twinges, but I've had nothing."

"No pain—nothing at all?"

Sarah shook her head. "And my due date was yesterday. Did I tell you that?"

"*Jah,* six times yesterday and several times over the past weeks."

Sarah's lips turned up just a little at the corners. "But it's the first time I mentioned it today. Florence says not to worry about anything; everything's perfectly normal." It was hard for Sarah not to worry. She had a feeling within that all would go well and her baby would be healthy, but what if she was wrong?

"See? So stop worrying. Start smiling. You'll soon have a beautiful *boppli* in your arms." Matilda jumped to her feet, then leaned down and tapped on the letter. "Open that. I'm certain you're worried about nothing."

"I will. And *denke,* for everything, Matilda."

Matilda leaned down and kissed Sarah on her forehead. "Everything will work out fine, you'll see. Don't get up. I'll see myself out."

Once again Sarah was alone. Before she'd

met Joel, she was alone most of the time. Her mother had died first and soon after, her father had followed. As much as she detested being alone, she'd grown used to it.

Now tired, Sarah closed her eyes and listened to the distant hoofbeats of her friend's buggy horse as they gradually grew fainter. Soon nothing but silence filled her house. She reached out and grabbed a blanket from the back of the couch and pulled it over herself. It was comforting to be wrapped in something soft and warm.

Often Sarah wondered how God chose some to have hardships while others seemed able to breeze through life with no concerns at all. To ask someone or to talk about things like that would make her seem petty and selfish. It was thoughts like these that Sarah kept to herself. Things seemed so easy for Matilda, who'd married Tom within two months of meeting him. Four children had arrived one after the other, and now Matilda was one person Sarah knew who had a perfect life.

She wasn't envious of Matilda or anyone else. It would just be nice for some happiness to come her way. Joel and she had been in love, but they had endured hardships, and Joel had been so pleased that their baby was coming, a *boppli* who would bring both of them great joy and happiness, but Joel would never see their baby in this life. They would meet in God's house when the day was done.

IT WAS dark when Sarah woke up from her sudden nap, and several hours had passed. The fire had gone out and it was the cold that had awakened her. If Joel were still alive, she would've cooked a meal and they would be sitting by each other on the couch in front of a raging fire. Life was definitely better when it was shared. After Sarah had rubbed her eyes, she pulled the blanket tighter around her and, after she had lit the gas lantern beside her, she made her way into the kitchen. It was too late to bother with lighting the fire now. A quick meal and an early night were what she decided on.

CHAPTER 2

*As for God, his way is perfect; the word of the
Lord is tried: he is a buckler to all them
that trust in him.*
2 Samuel 22:31

MATILDA CAME AT EXACTLY the same time the
next day and, as Sarah knew she would, the
first thing she did was reprimand her for not
opening the pesky envelope from the day
before.

Matilda slumped into the couch next to Sarah. "Don't tell me you haven't opened that yet?"

Sarah pouted, staring at the envelope. "I nearly did earlier. I'm getting around to it."

Matilda reached out and took up the envelope. "Whatever it is, you should know about it. There's no point burying your head in the sand. If it is another bill, just put it with the others. Don't let it stress you. I can call all the people you owe money to and work out a payment plan with them."

"What with? I have no income except a little sewing income, and I haven't been doing much of that of late. And I won't be able to do much after the *boppli's* born."

"Then that's what I shall tell the companies."

"I've considered it and there's little point to opening it. I've got little left. Whoever wants money now will just have to wait. Just like I'm waiting for my *boppli*. When he wants to come, he'll come. When I get money, they'll get money."

"I don't think it's the same thing. I don't think you can compare waiting for money to waiting for a birth."

"Probably not."

"Why don't I open it for you? If it's really bad, I'll just put back in the envelope and I won't mention it again. I'll just put it in the pile with the others. If it's only a small bill, Tom and I can help you out."

"I can't ask that."

"I offered, you didn't ask."

Sarah stared at her friend, hating the position she was in.

"I'm going to open it right now," Matilda said.

Sarah sighed again. "Okay. Open it quickly and if it's bad don't tell me."

Through gaps between the fingers now

covering her face, Sarah watched Matilda carefully put her fingernail under the flap and lift the fold just enough so she was able to rip the top of the envelope open. When she pulled the contents out Sarah saw that it was one piece of paper. It didn't look like a bill. It had to be a letter from someone since Matilda was now reading it and hadn't put it back down. It couldn't have been a bad bill or a letter of demand for payment of a bill."

"This is not a bill."

"That's a relief. Who's it from?"

"I'm still reading it."

She dropped the envelope into her lap as she grabbed each side of the page with her hands. Her eyes were round like saucers as she stared at Sarah. "You won't believe it!"

"What? What is it?"

"It's from a lady called Nellie and she's a friend of your *onkel* from Sugarcreek."

"I remember him. He's *Dat's bruder*, *Onkel* Harold. I visited him when I was a little girl. He died a couple of weeks ago. Didn't I tell you that? I couldn't even afford to go to his funeral." Sarah wondered why Matilda had gone quiet. Was Nellie reprimanding her for not going to the funeral? It would only be natural for *Onkel* Harold's friend to want a family member there. "I feel dreadful. I'll write to her and explain why I couldn't go, now that she's written to me."

"*Nee,* Sarah, you don't understand. It's not about that. She's saying your *onkel* has left you his farm. He had a share farm and a house, a buggy and a horse. It's all yours now! Sarah, it's all yours!"

Sarah stared at Matilda, not able to take it in.

"Nellie said her husband is helping to look after your *onkel's* estate and handling his affairs until you get there."

Her fingertips flew to her mouth. "Get there? I can't go anywhere with the *boppli*

17

coming. Matilda, there must be some mistake."

"*Nee,* there's no mistake. You now own a farm and a *haus.*"

"*Nee,* it can't be real. I can't believe such a thing."

"It's all true. The papers are waiting for you to sign, and then you'll own it free and clear. Here, read it for yourself."

"I can't. You read it out loud to me."

Sarah listened while Matilda read the description of all that she'd inherited from Harold.

Matilda placed the letter on the table in front of them. "You can sell the farm and buy something here."

"I'll go there to live, I think. I feel like I need a new start. There are too many sad memories here. This is perfect. But do you think it's all true? I can't take it in; it doesn't seem real."

"I can't think the woman would lie

about something like that. Your *onkel* died, and who else would he have left his things to?"

"A friend? He had no other relatives. I know *Dat* only had his *bruder,* Harold. And he'd never married, so there were no *kinner* to be my cousins."

"She's put her phone number at the bottom of the page. Why don't we call her now and talk to her?"

"Okay, let's do it. And then we'll know whether it's real."

Together they walked outside to use the phone in the barn, which was soon to be disconnected.

"You dial, Matilda. I'm too nervous."

Minutes later, Sarah was talking to Nellie, who told her she had a big house to live in, a *grossdaddi haus* for rental income, and the farm which made good money. Nellie went on to tell her that she had been a good friend of Harold's.

"I'll be there at the end of the month," Sarah said to Nellie.

As soon as Sarah replaced the receiver on the phone, Matilda said, "Didn't I tell you all your problems would soon be over? I didn't know it would be this soon, though. It reminds me of the story in the bible about the starving men who had no money, and they thought they were going to die, so they walked to the nearby town where the invading enemy had encamped, figuring it would be better to be prisoners."

"I know the story. *Gott* had sent a loud noise over the city, and the enemies had fled in terror. The men entered the vacated city and found food and great riches. They hid treasures for themselves, before realizing the right thing was to report to their king and let the bounty be shared amongst the people. *Gott* turned things around for them in one day."

"He's done the same for you, Sarah."

Sarah sat down on a bale of hay and tears flowed down her face. She thanked God for providing, but she couldn't help wondering why Joel had to be taken away. Couldn't he have shared in this too? She stared at the beams of light shining into the barn from the holes in the roof. Death had taken her husband away, and death had now provided for her and her child. Life indeed was a cycle, as the bishop always said.

Matilda kneeled down by her. "What are you thinking about, Sarah? You go so quiet sometimes."

Sarah knew she wasn't good at talking, since she was used to being on her own. She shared her inner thoughts with Matilda.

"We can't know why *Gott* does things, Sarah. His ways are higher than ours and we can't begin to know His thoughts. Maybe He's tested you and you passed the test."

"I don't want to be tested. I'm not strong enough."

Matilda leaned forward and wrapped her arms around her friend. *"Jah* you are, because *Gott* is giving you strength day by day, all that you need to handle this test. It's selfish of me, but I hope you don't go, but if you do I'll always be your very best friend."

"Denke, Matilda. You're the best!" Sarah placed her arm around her friend and returned the hug. "If I leave, I'll write all the time. I'll never forget you, and we can visit each other."

"Gott answers our prayers."

"He does, and it seems too good to be true."

"Believe it."

"Say you'll come and visit me?"

"I'll visit you and I'll write to you every week."

"Ah, but will you help me up?" Sarah held out her hands to be pulled out of the couch.

Matilda stood up, giggling, and then helped Sarah to her feet.

Sarah placed her hand over her tummy "Do you hear that, my *boppli?* We've been blessed with a place to live and an income from a farm."

Right at that moment, Sarah's water broke.

CHAPTER 3

Now faith is the substance of things hoped for,
the evidence of things not seen.
Hebrews 11:1

THAT NIGHT, a baby girl was born to Sarah
Kurtz. The tiny baby with dark hair and dark
blue eyes was named Gretel after Sarah's late
mother.

Matilda had stayed with her the whole
time, assisting the midwife. After the mid-

wife had left, Matilda lay down in bed next to her, exhausted. "It was tough work watching you give birth."

"Not as tough as the time I was having, I can tell you that. And that's the last time you'll hear me complain about anything. Apart from being exhausted, I'm feeling so blessed right now that I could burst."

"I know how you feel. I was like that when each of my boys arrived."

"*Denke* for putting up with me being so horrid lately."

"*Nee,* we all go through tough times. And you've been through a terrible upheaval with Joel going unexpectedly in the way that he did."

"I know. It was such a shock. If he'd been sick or something at least I might have been prepared for it. There I go, complaining again." She stared down at the bundle asleep across her chest. "Look at her sleeping so peacefully with not a care in the world. I want her to be this way forever —content."

"You should try to get some sleep now that Gretel is sleeping. It's easier if you do that the first few weeks. Sleep when she sleeps. The idea about sleeping in one big slab at night, throw it right out the window."

"Okay. I'll try. I'm exhausted, but I'm also excited. I hope I can sleep."

"You won't have to take in sewing any-more to make ends meet."

"I know, I can concentrate on making a nice happy home for Gretel. Are you staying the night?" When there was no answer, she turned to see that her best friend was already fast asleep. She held Gretel firmly against her, stood up, and placed her baby in her crib. After she had covered Gretel in another blanket, she crawled back into bed next to Matilda who stayed fast asleep.

"*Denke Gott,*" she whispered, "and *denke, Onkel* Harold."

. . .

MATILDA HAD BEEN THERE every day while her children were at school, and today Sarah was feeling well enough to finally make some real plans about traveling to Sugarcreek.

"*Denke Onkel* Harold," Sarah said aloud in front of Matilda. "And *denke Gott,*" she added in case Matilda would remind her that's where her blessing came from.

"*Jah,* it's sad that he's not going to be around, but him going to *Gott* right now was good timing for you and Gretel. Did you know your *Onkel* Harold well?"

"My *vadder* was very close with him. They kept in touch quite often. I remember visiting him when I was little, and then I don't have much memory except that he was a kind man who liked children even though he didn't have any of his own."

Matilda poured out a cup of tea for

Sarah.

"I'll have to start making plans. Like—how will I get there, for a start? I don't even know if there's a bus or a train or what?"

"Sugarcreek?"

"Jah. Would there be a bus or a train?"

"I think it's about six hours' drive away, and longer by train or bus, or whatever. Everywhere's always longer than it is by car. I'll have Tom find out for you what's the best way to get there."

"Would you? That would be *wunderbaar.* I'll need to write back to Nellie and tell her when I'm coming. I've given her a rough idea when I spoke to her on the phone last, but I think it's always best to confirm things in writing."

"Do you think you'll leave in about a fortnight?"

"I'll have to because that's when the rent runs out. I'm paid up for another two weeks. I've got so many things to do."

"Tom and I will help with everything."

"Denke. I never dreamed a year ago that I'd be sitting here with a baby in my arms and Joel not here."

"Life's like that sometimes—full of surprises."

"I wonder if this girl will ever have a *vadder.*"

"Would you consider marrying again?"

"I would. I liked being married and having someone with me all the time, and this girl needs a *vadder* and more siblings. I don't want her to be an only child like I was. And that doesn't mean I love Joel any less. I just don't want to be on my own, with just me and Gretel. We'd both be lonely."

"Of course not. I know you don't love Joel any less by wanting those things."

"I know *Gott* will find someone for me at just the right time, like He found us the house."

"And the income from the farm. You're totally set for life."

Sarah smiled at the thought of it. Such a heavy burden had been lifted from her shoulders.

That had been a pattern in Sarah's life; whenever she thought she couldn't take any more, God raised her out of the hard times. When she had been at the lowest point of her younger life, God had arranged for her to meet Joel. Now she'd felt even lower, and *Gott* had used *Onkel* Harold to meet her needs.

THE NEXT DAY Matilda arrived with good news. "All the arrangements have been made. Tom has found someone to drive you to Sugarcreek.

"Drive me all the way there? Won't that be expensive?"

"*Nee.* The man's a traveling salesman.

31

Tom has known him for many years. He travels around the countryside, and he's going to Ohio in two weeks time. Everything is falling into place perfectly."

"And he doesn't mind driving me and Gretel?"

"He said he'd be happy to do it. Tom offered to pay his gas money, but the man said no need because he was going that way anyway."

"*Denke,* Matilda. You and Tom have come through for me again. Can I organize everything in that time?"

"Yes, because you won't be doing it alone. I'll help you, and so will the ladies."

Sarah smiled at the baby in her arms. "Everything is working out perfectly. My baby and I will have a new life in Sugarcreek. I never for one moment imagined that I'd be leaving here, but I must go where *Gott* wants me to go."

CHAPTER 4

Delight thyself also in the Lord:
and he shall give thee the desires of thine heart.
Commit thy way unto the Lord;
trust also in him; and he shall bring it to pass.
Psalm 37:4-5

NELLIE HAD SUGGESTED that Sarah be driven to her house, as it was easier to find than *Onkel* Harold's farm.

As the salesman parked his car beside

Nellie's house, a woman came running out. Matilda guessed she was a little older than herself. Nellie had a kind face and Sarah liked her immediately. The man who drove her there pulled her bags out of the back as Sarah thanked him profusely. Nellie's husband, Seth, came out to greet her, took charge of the luggage and added his thanks before the man drove away.

"You must be exhausted. Come inside and have something to eat before we take you to the farm," Nellie said taking Sarah's baby from her arms.

Sarah sat down while Nellie and Seth told her all about the local community. Nellie then listed all the people, and who would be likely to become her friends going by age.

"And how many *kinner* do you have?" Sarah asked them. "We never got around to talking about that on the phone."

"*Gott* has blessed us with two boys. They

are in *schul* right now. They're ten and eleven. Mark and Matthew."

"Did Nellie explain to you about the farm income?" Seth asked.

"A little."

Nellie frowned at Seth while still hugging the baby who was asleep. "Don't talk about that now. Let her settle in first. There's enough time for all that later."

"It's not something you have to worry about. It's all been put in place. With the help of Joshua Byler. "

Nellie tapped her husband's arm telling him to be quiet. "I've told her all she needs to know for the moment."

"You mentioned that there's a horse and buggy? I'll need to be able to get around."

"*Jah.* And all your *onkel's* furniture is still there in the *haus,* but we've packed his personal things into boxes and put them in a corner of the barn. You can go through them as you have time, and see what you want to keep."

"*Denke* that's very good of you. My *onkel* and my *vadder* were very close."

"Harold often used to talk about your *vadder* and what they got up to when they were younger," Seth said.

"They enjoyed their childhood together. They were close in age," Sarah said.

"*Jah,* they weren't only brothers, they were friends," Nellie said.

Sarah nodded. "And is Harold's place far away?"

"It's your place now. You signed those papers and sent them back to the lawyers, didn't you?" Nellie asked.

Sarah giggled. "*Jah,* I did. It just seems funny to think of the place as mine. And I haven't even seen it since I was a little girl."

"Are you ready to see it now?" Seth asked.

"I certainly am. This is a new start for Gretel and me. And I can tell you that it couldn't have come at a better time. I had just paid the last of my money for rent, and then I didn't know what I was going to do."

"*Gott* always provides," Seth said with a twinkle in his pale blue eyes.

Sarah nodded. "He always does."

Seth smiled. "Weeping lasts for a night, but joy comes in the morning. Now, I've got all your luggage in the buggy and I'm ready to go when you are."

AS THE BUGGY clip-clopped along the narrow tree-lined roads, Nellie pointed out the houses they passed and informed Sarah who lived in each one.

The next farm they came to had an attractive white house with a red roof.

"And of course, you'll meet your neighbor, Joshua Byler. He's a widower with two *kinner,* a boy and a girl. His wife died some years ago and the children are just delightful."

Sarah's interest was piqued. She couldn't help but wonder if *Gott* had brought her all that way to meet another man—a widower with two children sounded perfect. *Marrying a widower would be good,* Sarah considered because he would understand how it felt to lose someone and he wouldn't be jealous that she couldn't just forget Joel.

"Well, here we are," Seth said as they headed up a driveway through double open gates.

"It's not far from your place at all," Sarah said, pleased that she knew people who lived so close.

"Visit us whenever you want, and let us know if you need anything. It takes a while to settle into a new place."

Sarah stepped out of the buggy with Gretel asleep in her arms. Nellie hurried in front and fished the key from behind a chair on the porch.

When Nellie picked up the key, she said, "That's where Harold always kept the key if he ever locked the place. Do you want me to show you through, or do you want to explore the place for yourself?"

"I don't want to keep you." She glanced behind her at Seth who was busy unloading her luggage.

Nellie also glanced at her husband. "Take all those suitcases up to the main bedroom, would you, Seth?"

"Of course."

"Does it all go to the bedroom?" Nellie asked Sarah.

"*Jah.* Can I offer you some tea? Oh, I don't even know if there's anything here."

"I did some shopping for you. There's enough of everything for a few days and there are chickens in a coop behind the barn." She pointed over at the large red barn.

"Chickens? That's lovely. I haven't kept chickens for a while. I miss them. The ones I had were raised from babies. They were my pets."

Nellie chuckled. "We won't stay, Sarah. *Denke* for asking us. The bay horse in the paddock there is your buggy horse and you'll find the buggy and the feed for the livestock in the barn."

Seth came down the stairs for the second load of luggage.

"I want to thank you for looking after everything and helping me come this far."

"It was a pleasure," Seth said.

Sarah looked around the house. "This looks very much like the house I grew up in. I do hope one day it might be filled with *kinner*."

"If *Gott* wills," Nellie cautioned, raising her eyebrows.

"*Jah,* of course. If *Gott* wills it."

Seth trudged downstairs after the second

round of taking luggage up to the bedroom, looking a little out of breath.

"*Denke,* for doing that Seth."

He smiled. "You'll find everything you need is here, and if not, there's a phone in the barn and Harold had a book with everyone's number written down. We made sure our number is in there for you."

"Don't hesitate to call us," Nellie added.

"This Sunday the gathering is on at the Wilsons' *haus.* That's the *haus* we showed you that's next to ours."

"*Jah,* I remember the one."

"Don't come if you're too tired. You've had a long journey."

"I'll have Friday and Saturday to rest. I should be fine. I'm looking forward to meeting everyone."

"And everyone's keen to welcome you, too," Seth said.

"Oh, I put the crib that I used for my boys upstairs with fresh linen in it."

"*Denke.* That helps me so much. I couldn't bring anything like that with me."

Gretel opened her eyes and started crying.

Nellie leaned forward and stroked Gretel on her cheek. "Such a beautiful *boppli.* We'll leave you to it, Sarah. Would you like me to come back tomorrow to help you unpack?"

"*Nee,* I'll be fine. There's not much to unpack; just a few clothes."

"I'll be back in a day or two, then, to see that you're settling in."

"*Denke,* Nellie."

Seth and Nellie hurried to the buggy. Sarah rocked Gretel back and forward, watching the buggy until it was out of sight.

CHAPTER 5

The Lord is my strength and my shield;
my heart trusted in him, and I am helped:
therefore my heart greatly rejoiceth;
and with my song will I praise him.
Psalm 28:7

"LET'S GO INSIDE, Gretel. I guess you need to be fed about now."

After Sarah had fed her, Gretel went right back to sleep. Sarah set about exploring her new house. The first thing she explored was the kitchen. It was large, with many cupboards and it had a huge utility room off from it. She leaned over the double sink and looked out the window. From there she had a good view of the farm and she could see the chicken coop.

When she was putting some vegetables on for dinner, she came across a bunch of keys next to the cupboard the potatoes were in. The label told her they were keys belonging to the *grossdaddi haus*. Knowing it would soon be dark, she decided to take a quick look at it in the daylight. Not wanting to leave Gretel alone in the house, she picked her up and took her with her.

As she walked around the side of the house, she wondered how much someone would pay to live in a *grossdaddi haus*. "Depends on how big it is, I suppose, and how many bedrooms," she murmured to herself.

Standing at the front door, she examined

the keys to see which one might fit. It was a large keyhole, so she tried the largest key. After it had clicked with no trouble, she pushed the door open and stepped inside.

"Who are you?" a startled-sounding voice from within yelled.

Sarah looked up, momentarily stunned to see an Amish man in his thirties.

"Who are *you*?" she shot back. "And what are you doing in my *haus*?"

"I live here."

"This is my *haus*."

"Oh. So you're Sarah Graber?"

"I'm Sarah Kurtz. Graber was my maiden name."

"Of course. Sarah Kurtz. I did hear about your husband, and I'm sorry."

She shook her head. "What are you doing here? I don't understand who you are."

He stepped closer. "Your *onkel* said I was welcome to stay here as long as I want."

Now she understood. This man was trying

to take advantage of her. She shouldn't have waited so long before she came. It was never good to leave a place vacant. He must've seen no one was living there and moved right on in. "Well, I'm the new owner. Not my *onkel.*"

He frowned at her.

"You have to leave. I didn't promise you anything even if my *onkel* did, which is doubtful." She knew she sounded rude, but she needed the income from the place. Going back to being poor was not something she was willing to do. This place was her future—hers and Gretel's.

"You've got that big *haus* to live in, and I'm told it's just you and your *boppli.* Why are you so keen on having me leave?"

"I need to lease this to a paying person."

"Ah, if that's the only problem I can pay you."

She narrowed her eyes wondering if he was bluffing his way through. "You can?"

"*Jah,* but not right now."

That's what she figured. "Why can't you pay now?"

"I'm waiting for money to come through. And you'll get enough money from the farming anyway. You don't really need money from leasing this place."

She frowned at him. "What do you mean?"

"I know how much Harold got from the share farm. He told me. I helped him with his finances. There'll be enough for you and your *boppli* to live off without the rent from this place."

Her mouth opened in shock. "That's none of your concern."

"I'm helping you work things out, seeing you must've just arrived today."

"I don't need any help. I'm quite capable of working things out for myself. I'm not stupid."

"I didn't say you were stupid, but you are a woman."

Her mouth fell open in shock. "So being a woman that's... that's a step up from stupidity in your mind?"

"That's not what I meant. Sometimes a man needs to point things out to a woman. Women needed to be guided by men, and since your man isn't around anymore..."

"Stop right there! Don't say anything else. And don't talk about my husband." She breathed out heavily, scarcely believing her ears. The man was annoying and rude, but at the same time, he had no money and if she kicked him out where would he go? Compassion pricked her heart. She had been nearly homeless, and God in His mercy had pulled her out of it. "And do you mind telling me where the money is coming from—the money you're waiting on?"

"I sold a property and I'll get the money as soon as it closes."

"And you don't work?"

"I do, well, I did. I was a construction worker and I can't do that anymore since I hurt my back. I've bought a business, but that doesn't finalize until after Christmas as well. The old owners wanted one more Christmas before I take over. It's a building supplies business."

She nodded. "It seems as though everything's happening for you after Christmas."

"Look, if you let us stay here, I'll pay you whatever you want once my money comes through. Then we'll leave. I'm a man of my word."

"Do you have other people staying with you?"

He looked confused.

"You said, 'us.' Do you have other people staying here?"

"Oh, that's my *kinner.* They're outside playing in the fields somewhere. They usually come home at dusk."

"There's no Mrs...."

He looked away. "She died."

"I'm very sorry to hear that. The one thing I'm concerned about, other than the money, is that it's not proper for a single man and woman to be living so close."

He looked at her as though she was stupid. "We're not! You're in that *haus,* and I'm here with my *kinner.* I can assure you that your virtue will be quite safe with me."

"I don't think the bishop would see things that way."

"He does. I talked about it with him before you arrived. He's my cousin."

"You asked him, and no one thought to ask me?"

"Didn't Nellie and Seth mention me at all? I was sure they would've."

"*Nee,* they didn't. What is your name? You haven't told me."

"I'm Joshua Byler."

"Oh, that's you?"

He nodded. "That's me."

"They did mention you were my neighbor, but I thought you lived in the house next door and I thought the *grossdaddi haus* was vacant. I assumed it was, because Nellie said it could be a rental, and no one mentioned that you were living here."

"Look, Mrs. Kurtz. It makes no difference whether I pay or someone else pays the rent, does it? My cousin can tell you I'm reliable and my word is good."

"Your cousin the bishop?"

"Jah. I'll pay you as soon as my money comes through."

She slowly nodded, but did so begrudgingly. Now she'd have to wait months for her money and he didn't seem to consider that she was doing him a big favor. Never would she have turned him and his children away, but there was something dislikable about the man. He seemed controlling, and it didn't sit well with her when people tried to push her around and treat her as though she was stupid.

"*Denke.* How old's the little one?"

"Two weeks."

"She's tiny."

"*Bopplis* generally are."

He chuckled. "What's her name?"

"Gretel."

"That's an unusual choice."

"After my *Mamm.* Gretel was her name, and I miss her. I have vegetables on. I'll probably see you tomorrow or something." Sarah took two steps back, turned, and then she was out the door. Hurrying back home, she hoped that the people leasing different sections of the farm were actually paying money or otherwise, she could be in trouble. After she had popped her sleeping baby down on the lounge and surrounded her with cushions to prevent her from rolling, she hurried to check the vegetables. They were only just simmering. She turned the heat up and stepped to the side and stared out the window at the lush green fields.

While she stared at the land that she now owned, she did her best to push aside her fear of having no money. When she had gotten the letter about inheriting the house and the farm she'd thought her years of lack were behind her, but after meeting that rude man, fear of lack had crept back in.

Surely God wouldn't have brought her all this way so she could end up broke once more. Swallowing hard, she told herself she was being silly and the man living in her *grossdaddi haus* was just a small setback, nothing in the scheme of things, if what she'd been told about the farming income was true.

Sarah sat down at the kitchen table amused at her recent daydreaming about the widower Nellie had mentioned. She'd imagined a perfect life with someone she hadn't met and when she had met him, he was someone she would never imagine herself tolerating. He was rude, opinionated, and bossy. What a pity his personality was enveloped in a strong-looking handsome man. His skin was lightly tanned, his dark hair framed his face nicely while his striking green eyes were fringed with long dark lashes.

When she heard giggling, Sarah sprang to her feet and looked out the window to see a boy and a girl near the chickens, running toward the house. They looked like nice happy children just like Nellie had said. If only someone had warned her that someone was in the *grossdaddi haus* it wouldn't have been such a shock.

AFTER DINNER, she took her baby up the stairs. She'd unpacked one bag that had enough clothes to last a few days. Once she placed Gretel in the crib that Nellie had generously loaned her, she pulled out the one set of sheets she'd brought with her and made up the double bed. She'd seen linens in the hallway closet while exploring the house, but thought that they might need to be laundered or aired out before she used them.

"*Gut nacht,* Gretel." She leaned over and kissed her baby lightly on her forehead.

She slipped between the sheets. Her head and her body still felt like she was in that moving car. What she needed was a good sleep, and she hoped that Gretel wouldn't wake up too many times during the night.

CHAPTER 6

Cast thy burden upon the Lord, and he shall sustain thee:
he shall never suffer the righteous to be moved.
Psalm 55:22

WHEN THE SUN streamed into the bedroom, Sarah was pleased that Gretel had only woken once in the night and had gone right back to sleep after a feeding and a diaper change.

What she needed now was a good breakfast of eggs. She found a basket in one of the kitchen cupboards and opened the front door to head out to the chickens. Stopping still after she opened the door, she looked down at her feet to see a basket of eggs. She looked around and saw no one who had left them there.

It had to have come from Joshua next door. Perhaps she'd been too harsh on him. Later that morning, she heard children giggling again and looked out the window. They were walking to the barn with their father. When they were out of sight, Sarah moved to another window to watch them. Joshua wheeled the buggy out of the barn, and then led his horse out. His horse was a fine-looking tall bay. He had the children help him hitch the buggy and then they all got in and drove away. He had to have been driving the children to school and she wondered if he'd come straight back to the *haus* or go somewhere else. If he wasn't working, where would he go?

Perhaps the eggs were a sign that he was sorry for how he acted the day before, and for how rude he'd been. Well, if he was willing to try to get along better then so would she.

After she had finished breakfast, she hurried upstairs, hearing Gretel's waking-up whimpers. As she changed Gretel's diaper, she told her baby all about the man and how rude he'd been. Then she told her daughter that she was going to go out of her way to show him that she was a friendly person. Yesterday she'd been tired and shocked, and might have been a little grumpy with him.

"Your *mudder* is not normally a grumpy person," she explained to Gretel. "Only when I'm tired, and we had a big day of driving yesterday and that always tires me out."

Gretel and she followed their normal routine of bath, another feeding and another diaper change. After that, Sarah heard the buggy return. When she saw Joshua alone and unhitching the buggy, she knew he was back to stay for a few hours, at least.

"Why don't we make our neighbor a cup of *kaffe* as a peace offering? We'll take it to him."

Gretel had found her fist and was sucking on it.

"You agree? Okay, let's do it."

When she had made the coffee, she carefully positioned the baby across one arm and picked up the coffee with her other hand. She walked out to the front door, placed the coffee down on a nearby table, opened the door, picked up the cup and walked through the door, leaving it open behind her. As she reached the *grossdaddi haus,* she was pleased to see that the door was ajar.

"Hello," she called out.

The door was suddenly pulled wide open. "*Jah?*"

She smiled at him putting on her best friendly face. "Hi, I brought you some *kaffe.*"

He frowned at her. "I can boil water here. I have a gas stove."

"It's my way of... I feel we might have gotten off on the wrong foot."

"And that's fixed by bringing me a cup of *kaffe?*"

Now she could see that it hadn't just been her tiredness that had made things difficult. *He* was the problem, not she.

"Mrs. Kurtz, an apology will do."

"Apology for what?"

"Here, let me take that hot *kaffe.* You really shouldn't have the boiling hot drink near the *boppli.*"

He took the mug from her.

"You think I've got something to apologize for?"

"Don't you? You just said so now yourself."

Her eyes grew wide at the nerve of the

man putting words into her mouth. He'd been the rude one. Now he was being even ruder.

"Enjoy the *kaffe*," she said as she turned away from him.

"I don't want it," he called after her.

She checked her temper, stopped, and went back to him. "It was nice of you to put the eggs at my front door."

"That wasn't me. That was my son. He's thoughtful like that."

"You've been making use of the eggs?"

"I have, otherwise, they would've gone to waste. You can add the eggs to what I owe you. I calculate I owe you seven eggs a day. Add that to my account."

"*Nee,* that's not what I meant. I wouldn't do that." It seemed everything she said was making things worse. "Look, I'm trying to be friendly."

"We are being cordial, aren't we? We're just discussing business, but I'm used to talking business with men. Women are far too emotional, it seems."

"Are you saying that, if I was a man, I'd charge you for the eggs you've used so far?"

"That would make the most sense."

"You're making things very difficult."

He rubbed his chin and the muscles around his mouth tightened. "I'm sorry. What would you like me to say? You tell me and I'll say it."

Sarah grunted loudly. "You're hard to get along with."

"While we're talking, I need to discuss my *kinner* with you. They like looking after the chickens; would you like them to continue while we're here?"

"*Jah,* if they like looking after them I don't want to take that away from them."

"Good. At least we agree on something."

"I might meet your *kinner* sometime later, I hope."

"Jah, I'll have them introduce themselves to you after *schul."*

"Okay." She backed out the door. "Sorry to disturb you. I just thought…"

"That's okay. We've discussed all that we needed to, haven't we?"

"I guess so. I'll leave you alone, then."

She walked out the door, annoyed with him for being rude about the coffee and acting like she was being reckless in regard to her daughter's safety. The hot drink was in her other hand and her baby was in no danger from it at all. The man clearly thought that women had no sense at all.

After she had placed Gretel in her crib, she walked around wondering if Joshua really had money coming through. If not, she might be stuck with him for a lot longer than Christmas.

Sarah did her best to stop thinking about Joshua and what she could do to get along with him. The coffee idea hadn't worked;

he'd just made her feel a fool for offering it. He was best left alone. Being close to homeless herself, she couldn't turn him and his two children away. She had to show him the mercy that God had shown her.

CHAPTER 7

I will lift up mine eyes unto the hills, from whence cometh my help.
My help cometh from the Lord, which made heaven and earth.
Psalm 121:1-2

SARAH HEARD Joshua's buggy horse clip-clopping up the driveway, and she opened the door hoping to meet the children. If she got along well with them, that might help her get along with their father. It was important not to get off on the wrong foot in her new community, and from what Joshua had said, he was the bishop's cousin. That was a big reason to find a way to peaceable life with him as her neighbor.

She watched Joshua say a couple of words to his children, and then she saw them leap from the buggy and hurry toward her.

"Hello, Mrs. Kurtz. I'm Benjamin and this is my little *schweschder,* Holly."

"Well, hello to the both of you. *Denke* for bringing me some eggs this morning. Your *vadder* tells me you like looking after the chickens."

"We've named them all," Holly said.

"I used to like looking after chickens when I was younger, too."

"You can help us," Holly said.

"I'd like that."

"*Dat* says you have a *boppli.* Can I see her?" Holly asked.

"She's sleeping, but if you be very quiet and if it's okay with your *vadder* you can come in for a while and see her."

"*Dat* can we have a look at Mrs. Kurtz's *boppli?*" Benjamin called out to his father.

"Okay, but be good and do what she tells you."

"We will, *Dat.*"

Sarah led the children to Gretel, who was sleeping on the couch.

"She's tiny," Benjamin said.

"Sooo tiny," Holly agreed. "Can I help you look after her?"

"*Nee*, Holly, she's too tiny to play with," her brother told her.

"When she gets a little older, she'd like you to play with her," Sarah said.

"I can help you with other things," Holly said.

"We'll see," Sarah said smiling at Holly's bright eyes so full of enthusiasm.

The children were both fair haired with

hazel eyes, quite unlike their father whose coloring was dark and whose eyes were green.

"Can we hold her?" Benjamin asked.

"Jah, when she wakes up you can hold her. If you sit very still, I can place her in your arms."

"Can we come back later and see if she's awake?" Benjamin asked.

"Jah. She should be awake soon."

"Denke, Mrs. Kurtz, for showing her to us," Holly said.

"She's so small," Benjamin commented again.

"So pretty," Holly added.

"We better go and help *Dat* with the buggy. He's hurt his back and he needs our help."

"Okay." Sarah walked back to the front door with the children. They ran to their father who was waiting by the buggy.

Sarah closed the door, and then moved to

the window to watch what happened next. It seemed it might have been true about his back if he was getting his children to help with hitching and unhitching the buggy. But when he had hitched it to go and collect them he hadn't needed their help.

He lifted his hand up and waved to her. When she realized he could see her, she gave an embarrassed little wave, and moved back from the window. The man was annoying at best, and at worst, he intended to stay on indefinitely. And if he stayed at the *grossdaddi haus* forever, there was nothing much she could do about it. She was pleased that the children were delightful and polite, just as Nellie had reported.

CHAPTER 8

Trust in the Lord with all thine heart;
and lean not unto thine own understanding.
In all thy ways acknowledge him, and he shall
direct thy paths.
Proverbs 3:5-6

EARLY SUNDAY MORNING, Sarah went out to hitch her buggy. She'd made sure it was all intact and working the previous afternoon.

"What are you doing?"

She swung around to see Joshua standing with his legs spread and hands on hips. His usual expression of disapproval was plastered on his face.

"I'm getting ready to go to the meeting."

"It makes no sense for us to go separately. You're coming with us. We're coming back here when it's finished, so it makes sense."

There he was, telling her what to do again. "I'll take my buggy; *denke* for the offer."

"You'll have to come with us."

She frowned. "And why is that?"

"Your horse is lame."

"He doesn't look lame in the least to me."

"Do you know anything about horses?"

He had her there. She didn't know a lot about horses. Joel had always looked after that side of things. Now she wished she had learned something about them. "*Nee,* but he looks fine to me."

He grumbled, "He's old and he's lame. He needs to be retired."

Sarah swallowed hard, not wanting it to be true. Did that mean she had to find money to buy a new horse? "Are you certain he's lame?"

"*Jah,* I am. I was telling Harold for some time that the horse was too old, but Harold rarely took him out. I mostly drove Harold everywhere."

Sarah nodded. This was not what she had been told. When she was told she had a horse and a buggy, she had assumed they would all be in perfect working order. "*Denke,* I'll go with you. I wouldn't want to drive a lame horse."

"It's the only sensible thing to do. I'll take you next week to look at another horse. There's an auction on Tuesday."

She shook her head. "I've no money at the moment."

"You should have money. Monday is the

last day of the month and that's when you get your money for the month. There'll be enough for you to live on, pay your bills and buy a buggy horse."

"Really? That much money?"

"*Jah.* I helped Harold with his finances and did his banking for him when he couldn't get out to do it himself. He's kept money aside for a new horse."

She heard her baby cry. "Do you need help hitching your buggy?"

"Benjamin and Holly always help me."

"I'll go and get Gretel."

"Okay. We'll be ready to go soon."

Sarah hurried to get her baby. She'd already had everything she needed for Gretel packed in a bag by the door. She scooped Gretel up, took hold of the bag and headed out to the buggy. By the time she got outside, the children were helping their father.

"*Gut mayrie,* Mrs. Kurtz," Benjamin said.

"Gut mayrie, Mrs. Kurtz," Holly said after her brother.

"Good morning to both of you," Sarah said.

"How is Gretel?" Benjamin asked.

"She had a good night and now she's sleeping again."

"Concentrate on what you're doing," their father said gruffly.

They turned their attention to hitching the buggy.

When they were ready, Sarah climbed up into the buggy next to Joshua and the children got into the back. She wondered how it was for them losing their mother when they were so young.

WHEN THEY ARRIVED at the house where the church was meeting, Joshua said, "You go on ahead. I'll park the buggy."

He let her and the children out.

"We'll show you into the house," Benjamin said.

"I'd like that, *denke*, since I don't know anyone yet."

The children took her to the people who owned the home, Mr. and Mrs. Wilson, before heading off to greet their friends. After she'd spoken with them for a few minutes, the Wilsons took her to meet the bishop.

"I'm sorry I haven't been out to greet you. My *fraa* and I would like to visit you tomorrow if you'll be home."

"I'd like that. *Jah*, I'll be home all day tomorrow." As soon as she said that, she remembered she'd intended to go and buy some food. She could still do so if they came early. "Would you be coming in the morning?"

"*Jah*, if that's better for you we could come at around nine."

"That would be perfect."

Sarah settled into a chair by the door, so

if Gretel cried she would be able to take her outside easily without having to climb over people.

She looked around to see where Joshua was. Through the open front door, she spotted Joshua walking to the house with a woman either side of him. They were looking at him with adoration and both women seemed to be talking at the same time. The women had to be unmarried, and they appeared to be around twenty or not much older.

When both women took their seats inside, Sarah looked around the room. There had to be a lack of single men in the community if women were flocking around her grouchy neighbor. His face was handsome, she begrudgingly admitted. Even though he was attractive to look at, he was disagreeable.

Once the house was full of people, the service began. The bishop gave a sermon on brotherly love and how people should treat others how they would like people to treat them. They were fitting words that spoke to Sarah's heart.

When the service was over, Sarah moved outside the house and the same two ladies she'd seen walking with Joshua hurried over to her and introduced themselves.

One was Sadie and one was Elizabeth.

"We heard that you've moved into Harold's old place," Sadie, the younger-looking of the two, said.

"That's right. Harold was my *onkel*. I moved here only a couple of days ago."

"Have you met many people yet?" Elizabeth asked.

"Only a few people."

"Did you know Joshua before you arrived?" Elizabeth asked, while the other woman seemed eager to learn the answer as well.

"*Nee.* I only met him a couple of days ago

when I got here." She wanted to ask why they were so keen on him, but he could've been nice to them. Perhaps she'd been too abrupt with Joshua when they first met and that had set the negative tone.

"Joshua tells us that you're a widow?"

"*Jah,* my husband died just a few months ago."

Sadie stared at Gretel and her mouth turned down at the corners. "And you've got this small *boppli.*"

"Do you have any other *kinner?*" Elizabeth asked.

"Just the one."

The women looked at each other as though they'd learned enough for now.

"Have both of you known Joshua for long?"

"I grew up here," said Sadie, "and Elizabeth moved here a while ago, after she visited our community for a wedding."

Sarah figured she might as well learn a

thing or two from them. "Did you know Joshua's *fraa?*"

"*Jah,* we did."

"We knew Katherine."

Elizabeth said, "Katherine was my first cousin."

"It was a shock to everyone that she died so young," Sadie said.

"Katherine was his *fraa?*" Sarah asked.

Sadie nodded. "It was a high fever that killed her."

"What was wrong with her?"

"She had pneumonia. She wasn't the only one who died from it that winter," Elizabeth explained.

"I'm so sorry to hear that. It's a dreadful loss for him and his two *kinner.*"

One of them leaned in. "They aren't really his. Katherine was a widow and married Joshua when the *kinner* were three and four. She died soon after."

"I never would've known. He treats them

as though they're his own." That did explain why they were so lovely, though, while he was crotchety.

"He's a *wunderbaar* man," Sadie said.

"He is," Elizabeth agreed.

"Here you are, Sarah. I was looking for you."

Sarah turned around to see Nellie.

The two girls made the excuse that they had to help with the food and hurried back to the house.

"I see you've met Sadie and Elizabeth."

"Jah. I did."

"I can guess what they were asking you about."

Sarah frowned not wanting to betray the girls' confidence or get drawn into gossip. "What do you think they were asking me?"

"About Joshua. It's no secret that they've both got huge crushes on him."

"Everyone knows?"

"Jah."

"Speaking of Joshua, I didn't know there was anyone actually living in the *grossdaddi haus.* When you mentioned him as being the neighbor, I thought you meant that he was living on the farm next door."

"Ach, Nee, I'm sorry. I thought I mentioned it. He's been living there for a good six months. He helped Harold with day-to-day living—paying bills and organizing his money. Seth and I helped with other things, and one of those things was his will and seeing that everything was just as he wanted."

"It seems everyone's got nothing but good things to say about Joshua."

"Does that surprise you?"

"Nee, but he's very forthright about things."

"He's had to be that way with everything that's happened to him."

"Jah, I heard about his wife dying and him hurting his back."

"It's just been one thing after another for poor Joshua."

"He's very kind, it seems. He's offered to take me to a horse auction on Tuesday to choose a new horse."

"He was always telling Harold he needed a new one, but Harold didn't want to spend the money—it seemed."

"Perhaps I shouldn't. Although Joshua said that Harold had put money aside for one."

"Did Joshua say you'd have enough money come end of month?"

"*Jah,* he did."

"He's the one who knows all about the finances of the farm. He helped Harold set it all up a couple of years ago. Before that, Harold had nothing, and Joshua encouraged him to set up the share farm and then Harold had money coming in."

"Joshua did that?" Just then, Gretel woke and started squirming. Sarah picked her up and placed her against her shoulder and patted her on the back to calm her while Nellie talked.

"He's helped so many people."

"I had no idea."

"Oh, he'd never tell you. He's not like that. He can be a little overbearing, like he's telling you what to do, but you just have to get used to him."

Sarah gave a little giggle out of nervousness. She wanted to ask why she had to get used to the way Joshua was. It sounded like he was going to be at her farm for a rather long time. Remaining quiet about the matter was what she decided to do; otherwise, people would get the wrong impression of her. First impressions counted a great deal.

Gretel started crying.

"Is there somewhere I can feed her?"

"Yes, you can go into one of the upstairs bedrooms. Come with me and I'll ask which one you can use."

. . .

SARAH SAT on the bed upstairs nursing her baby while she could hear nothing but buzz from half a dozen conversations happening below her. She was starting to get a more complete picture of Joshua. He was bossy and dominating because he'd had to take charge. He became both mother and father to the children when their mother died. And he seemed to make no distinction that they weren't his children by birth. And he'd helped Harold develop an income by organizing the share farm on land that Harold wasn't able to work alone given his advancing years.

It seemed that taking over was Joshua's way. Sarah smiled as she remembered his face when she'd brought him the mug of coffee a couple of days ago. He'd thought she was out of her mind. He was very much a plain and practical person. Now it bothered

Sarah that she'd spent the whole day thinking about why he was the way that he was.

"Your *mudder's* going quite mad, Gretel." Her baby kept right on feeding.

When Gretel was finished, she changed her diaper and went downstairs. The older people were leaving and the young people were staying on for the singing. Anxious that she'd made Joshua and the children wait for her, she looked around until she saw him and the children waiting by the buggy. She hurried over.

"I'm so sorry to keep you waiting. I was just feeding the baby and then she needed changing."

"That's okay. We're not in a hurry."

"Can I help with the *boppli* today when we get home?" Holly asked.

"I don't know that there's much to do today. I'll be doing some washing tomorrow, but you'll be at *schul* and she's a little young to play with."

"Don't bother, Mrs. Kurtz."

"Holly's no bother, Mr. Byler." She looked down at Holly. "You can come and help later today if you'd like. I'm certain there's something that you can do to help with Gretel."

"Can I, *Dat?*" Holly looked up at her *vadder.*

"If Mrs. Kurtz says you can then it's okay with me."

"*Denke, Dat,*" Holly said, "but don't I have chores at our house?"

"Sunday's a day of rest. We don't need to do anything today, Holly," Joshua reminded her. "We should be going now. It looks like we're going to get some rain and I'd like to get home before we do. Do you need help getting into the buggy?" Joshua asked Sarah.

"You can help with my bag."

"Benjamin, take Mrs. Kurtz's bag."

Benjamin did as he was asked.

Sarah, with Gretel in her arms, climbed into the buggy. When she got comfortable, she looked up to see Sadie and Elizabeth looking at the buggy and whispering. She hoped she wasn't going to become the subject of gossip. Everyone knew that they both lived on the same farm, so surely it had made sense to travel to the meeting together.

CHAPTER 9

*I will say of the Lord, He is my refuge and my
fortress:
my God; in him will I trust.*
Psalm 91:2

"YOU MUST FEEL COMFORTED HAVING Joshua living in the *grossdaddi haus*," Mary said on Monday morning, teacup in hand as she sat next to her husband, Bishop Peter, in Sarah's living room.

"I didn't know he was going to be there. No one told me, and I opened his door to look around the day I got here and there he was."

"He will look after the place."

"How? Hasn't he hurt his back?" Sarah asked.

"Jah, he did and now he can't do what he used to do, but he still helps everyone who asks him. Soon he's going to help someone with his old barn. The owner wants to tear it down and build a new one."

"And it's about time too. It was hit by lightening and half of it burned down and it's been like that for months."

"The old man is too old to fix it by himself. I told him the community will rebuild it, but he said he only needs a small barn. His idea is that his sons can help him knock it down and Joshua will give him ideas on what he'll need to build a new one."

"It sounds like Joshua is a valued member of the community."

"He is, and he's raising Katherine's *kinner* as his own even though Katherine's *schweschder* said she'd take them in."

"I suppose it was a good thing he hurt his back because now he's bought a business and he'll be able to be there more for them. If he was still working construction, that would be a sunup to sundown job," Bishop Peter explained.

"He takes over the business early next year?"

The bishop nodded. "That's right."

"It was a shock to everyone when Katherine died," Mary said shaking her head with eyes cast downward.

"It must've been awful for him."

She looked up at Sarah. "And you'd know a little about loss because you lost your husband young."

"I did."

"How did he die? If you don't mind me asking."

"I don't mind. Joel died while he was traveling by bus. He'd lost his job and one of his cousins said Joel could work for him. It would've meant he'd have to live away for a few months at a time, but that was the only job he could get and with the baby coming and everything, we needed the money. He went by bus to see about the job and on his way back the bus crashed."

"*Gott* must've wanted him home." Bishop Peter smiled kindly at her.

"I didn't, though. I wanted him to stay with me."

The bishop's gentle smile didn't falter. "His ways are higher than ours and we aren't to know why He calls someone home when He does."

"I know. That's what I keep telling myself, but sometimes I still wonder why..."

"You must trust, Sarah. Sometimes we're pulled into trials before we know it."

"Now you're here in the community with us, and now you have a home that's yours," Mary said.

Sarah nodded. "The house came at the right time. I only had a month left to go on the lease and then I was going to have to move in with another family."

"What you need is another husband. You're young enough."

Sarah smiled. "If that's in *Gott's* plan for me."

"We've got many single *menner* in the community," Mary said.

"Have you?"

"We'd have half a dozen, wouldn't we?" Bishop Peter asked his wife.

"*Jah,* and a couple of widowers, not counting Joshua, because he'll never marry again."

"Why won't he marry again? I thought

SAMANTHA PRICE

he'd be looking for someone to help raise
Benjamin and Holly."

"He's been on his own long enough. He
must like it or something. I only say that because he's had various opportunities and he's
passed them by."

"Would you like another cup of tea?"
Sarah asked.

"Just a quick one and then we'll have to
go," Mary said.

"Monday's our day for visiting. We don't
get many people moving into the community," Bishop Peter explained.

"We had Elizabeth move here last year,"
Mary corrected him.

"Is she a young woman?" Sarah asked. "I
was talking to someone called Elizabeth yesterday, but I don't remember her last name."

"Elizabeth Esh. She's a young woman,
and she's always with Sadie Yoder."

"*Jah,* I met them both at the same time at
the meeting."

"Elizabeth moved here after she came to her cousin's wedding. She immediately became friends with Sadie, and she moved in with Sadie and her parents."

"And are either of them getting married soon? They're about the marrying age aren't they?"

Mary shook her head. "They're a little past the normal marrying age. Elizabeth is twenty two and Sadie is twenty three."

Sarah recalled how they were both talking with Joshua. They both had crushes on him.

"So, you're settling in here well?"

"*Jah*, it's perfect. The *haus* is bigger than I'm used to, but I'm not complaining."

"It was Harold's *vadder's* home before him. That would be your *grossdaddi*."

"I remember meeting *Onkel* Harold when I was a little girl, but my *grossdaddi* had died by then. It's all a bit daunting, meeting new people and trying to work out who's who. I just have to settle in and then I'll be fine."

"*Gut.*"

"How are you getting along with Joshua?" Bishop Peter asked.

Sarah nodded. "Fine."

Mary leaned forward. "He'll be a help to you."

"He's been a good help already and tomorrow he's taking me to buy a buggy horse."

Bishop Peter nodded. "My cousin knows his horses."

"Someone told me that his children were his wife's from before. She was a widow and then he married her and she died shortly after."

"That's right. You'd never know he wasn't always their *vadder.*"

"I was shocked when I found that out. They just seem that they've always been together."

"I've got a cousin visiting next week and I was wondering if you might care to join us for dinner?" Mary asked. "We're actually going to be at Seth and Nellie's place for the meal."

"I'd love to join you for dinner."

"Wait. I have to tell you about him first. He's going around the communities looking for a suitable wife. I didn't know if you'd be interested in finding a husband so soon after yours has died."

"I've never liked to be alone, which is a funny thing because I'm an only child."

"Maybe that's actually why you don't like to be alone," the bishop pointed out.

"Perhaps." Sarah giggled. "What's he like?"

"I haven't seen him in years, so I can't really say. All I know about him is that he's a leatherworker. He is quiet and he hasn't been able to find a wife. His mother suggested he travel for a few months to meet some new people, so that's what he's doing.

Now, what do you say about meeting my cousin?"

"I'd love to, but wouldn't he want someone younger? I have Gretel too."

"There's only one way to find out—come to dinner. Joshua and his *kinner* will be there, too, as well as some other folk."

"Oh, I see."

"I thought it best to have a few people, otherwise, it would be too forced."

The bishop chuckled at his wife's words.

"I don't think I've met a leatherworker before," Sarah said, hoping she wasn't going to regret accepting the dinner invitation.

Mary's eyes traveled to Sarah's sewing in the corner of the room. "You like sewing?"

"I do. I used to sew for a living before I had Gretel."

"You should come and sew with the ladies. Every Thursday afternoon we have a quilting bee where we sew quilts to auction off to raise money for the volunteer fire-fighters."

"I'd love that. *Denke,* Mary." That was just what Sarah was looking for—a way to be included in the community.

"I can collect you and take you with me. We generally use Martha Sawtell's *haus* to meet at, and I drive right past your door."

"Thursday afternoon. I'll remember that."

CHAPTER 10

And the Lord God said, It is not good that the man should be alone; I will make him an help meet for him.
Genesis 2:18

ON TUESDAY MORNING after he had taken the children to school, Joshua was ready to take Sarah to buy herself a horse.

She stepped into his buggy with Gretel in her arms.

"I'll take you to the bank to get money out, unless you've got a wad of cash on you."

Sarah shook her head. *"Nee,* I don't. I'll need to go to the bank. I've got a little bit and that's all. How much will I need?"

"Take out two and a half thousand dollars."

She gasped. That seemed like an awful lot to spend on a horse. "I don't know that there'll be that much there."

"Harold's money has already gone into your account and he had enough for a buggy horse. I told you he'd been saving."

"And you're sure I need one? I don't want to be wasteful."

"You need one. I told you already the old one needs to be retired. A good horse should last you five to ten years." He clicked his horse onward toward the road.

Sarah nodded. "I'll take your advice."

"I'm only trying to help you."

"I know you are, and I appreciate it. I really do."

"Next stop is the bank, so you can take money out and see how much money you've got. Then you'll know that you can spend the proper amount on a horse."

"Okay *denke.* I'd feel better knowing that."

"And don't forget, you'll have money going into your account at the end of every month. So you'll need to budget for horse feed, household expenses and so on, but you will have enough."

"Denke. I'm aware of the need to budget my money. I don't go on spending frenzies." He was being helpful, but he was also treating her as though she were a ten-year-old child. She shifted in her seat, trying to avoid showing her annoyance. "It's nice of you to help me today."

He looked at her and smiled. "I'm happy to do it. Anything to look after Harold's niece."

"Your *kinner* are very helpful. They're bringing eggs to me every morning."

"They like to be helpful."

She kept quiet about the information she had on him, as it was the only polite thing to do.

After a peaceful buggy ride, he pulled up outside the bank and she got out.

"I'll park the buggy around the corner and then I'll come and find you."

"Okay."

She hurried into the bank and the teller told her how much money she had. It was more money than she'd ever had. She withdrew enough money for a horse, the teller passing it to her in an envelope, and she went outside to find where he'd parked the buggy. Joshua was standing there, right outside the bank waiting for her.

"That was fast," he said with a grin.

"I didn't want to keep you waiting."

"Was everything okay?"

"*Jah,* everything was as you said it was going to be. I took the cash out to buy the horse."

"*Gut.* I'll carry it for you."

"That's okay. I can mind it."

"It's easier if I look after it because I'll be doing the bidding for you."

She stared at him and he looked so concerned that she agreed. "Okay. If it matters that much, you can look after it."

"Sarah, it just makes sense, that's all."

She took ahold of Gretel with one arm while she passed Joshua the envelope. "There you are. I hope that buys me a horse."

"It will."

She decided to open up a little about her husband hoping that the awkwardness between them would begin to break down. "Joel always used to do these things for me."

"That's what men do."

And that was it. He'd shut her down with a single statement. She figured that there was nothing she could do or say to help them become better friends. Perhaps some people were never meant to be friends. At least he was helpful toward her and she was grateful for that.

As they walked back to the buggy, he said, "Now I have a surprise for you."

"You do?"

He nodded and smiled.

"I love surprises."

"We aren't going to an auction. I've already found a horse for you and all we have to do is pay for him and collect him."

She fixed her eyes on him and stopped in her tracks. "You've chosen my horse for me?"

He stopped still and stared back at her. *"Jah,* I asked around and checked out a few horses for you yesterday. I came across a real beauty with just the right temperament and he's an experienced buggy horse. He's perfect and he came at a good price."

"I wanted to choose my own."

"Nee, you didn't. You said you didn't know anything about them. That's why I was going to the auction with you."

She stared at him not believing he was shaking his head at her. Now he was trying to tell her what she wanted. "I did. I wanted to go to the horse auction and choose my own horse." Her voice showed an amount of force that she figured was necessary to get through to him.

"Sarah, you didn't. You told me you don't know anything about horses; that's why you wanted me to go with you," he repeated slowly as though he were speaking to a dis-obedient child.

"That part is true, but I imagined we'd be at the auction looking at a few horses and then I thought I'd be able to choose one from a small selection. Don't you see that?"

"There's no point doing that now. You wouldn't get a better horse than this one if you went to five auctions."

Sarah was irritated that he had gone ahead on this without letting her know. But if she carried on about it, she'd sound ungrateful and cranky, and she didn't want to be that way. "I appreciate you going to all that trouble to find me a *gut* horse."

He smiled gradually. "We'll go and collect him right now. His name is Snuffles, but you can change that if you want. That's what his old owners called him."

"Is he close by?"

"Five miles away. We can attach him to the buggy and lead him back."

For the first few minutes of the journey, Sarah was silent. She was fuming inside and still in shock over him buying a horse for her without her being there. Not even her husband would have made such big decisions without including her. It made her wonder what Joshua's wife had been like, to be able to put up with him. Perhaps they'd argued all the time.

"Tell me about the horse."

"There's not much to tell. He's an experienced buggy horse, which is important. He's proven himself. Some can seem all right, but it's no use if they're too nervous or excitable. Even a good horse could've been like that when it was younger. The experience is so important with all the traffic about these days. He's not just a horse straight from the racecourse. And he's sound as well, strong and healthy."

He pulled into a farm and stopped by a paddock.

"Whose farm is this?" she asked.

"Nathan Hostetler's farm. He's a cousin. It was his son's horse. Nathan bought it for his son, but his son and his new wife have moved away."

"I met so many people on Sunday. I don't even remember if I met him. His name sounds familiar."

"Nathan and Mary Hostetler."

"*Jah,* I'm sure I met them."

"You'll get to know everyone soon enough."

"Mary, I mean the bishop's wife, Mary, is having me go to a sewing afternoon with her on Thursday."

He made no comment, appearing uninterested in her social life, and he simply got out of the buggy. At least she was trying. She got out and followed him over to the fence. She had left Gretel in the seat, soundly sleeping and wrapped securely in a shawl, knowing that she was going to stay close by the buggy.

"There he is." He pointed to a black horse in the paddock.

"He looks good and so shiny."

"You wouldn't know a good one from a bad one, you told me."

"Well, be that as it may, he still looks good to me."

He walked back to the buggy, got a halter

and rope, and then opened the gate.

As he walked toward the horse, she called after him, "Do we just take him?"

"We can leave the money in his letterbox. The amount has been agreed upon." He kept walking toward the horse who was standing there watching them. The horse didn't flinch when he slipped the halter over his head.

"He seems nice and quiet." Her words were met with silence.

Joshua walked the horse through the gate and led him toward the buggy.

"Stop, Joshua. I'd like him to get to know me." She stepped forward and put out her hand for the horse to smell. "I will call him Midnight."

Midnight took a small step toward her.

"He approves of you."

"And I approve of him. He's very handsome."

"Is that what it takes to win you over?" He smirked at her.

"For a horse, maybe."

"Have we finished with the meet and greet?"

"Jah." She was pleased with herself for taking a tiny bit of control in the situation.

Then he clipped the lead onto the rear of the buggy.

"Shut the gate, will you?" he called out.

"Jah, of course." Once she'd shut the gate, she got back into the buggy, reached over to lift Gretel up and held her close.

Soon, he climbed in beside her.

"We don't have far to go to get home if that's what you were wondering."

"I was. I was hoping my *haus* was close by. I'm still working out where I am."

"We're only a mile away from home."

"Gut, denke."

At the end of the Hostetlers' driveway, he stopped by the letterbox, got out and placed the money inside.

CHAPTER 11

Be strong and of a good courage,
fear not, nor be afraid of them: for the LORD
thy God,
he it is that doth go with thee; he will not fail
thee, nor forsake thee.
Deuteronomy 31:6

WHEN THEY ARRIVED BACK at the house, he
unclipped the horse.

"What should I do with him now? Should he go into one of the stalls?"

"*Nee,* he'll be okay in the paddock. He's used to being in a paddock. We'll bring him in when the weather gets colder."

"What do you suggest I do with the old horse?"

"We can leave him where he is, or ask around to see if anyone wants a retired horse."

"That's it?"

"*Jah.*"

It was important to her to get on well with him and everyone here because this community was going to be her new family and this place was her new home. He'd made the effort to help her, so she would make the effort to be friendly.

"Would you, Holly and Benjamin like to come for dinner tonight? I have to thank you in some way."

"It's not necessary."

"You'd be doing me a favor. I like to cook for people."

He chuckled showing the first amount of warmth all day. "Holly and Benjamin would appreciate some proper cooking for a change. Cooking is not one of my better skills."

"*Wunderbaar.* Shall I expect you at about six?"

"That would be good."

With her baby in her arms, she watched him turn the horse out into the paddock.

He stood there and watched the horse for a moment before he turned back around. "I'll give him some food. That'll make him feel at home."

"Okay, *denke.*" Sarah walked back into her house and wondered what to cook for dinner. When Nellie had stopped by the day before, she had driven her to the store, so she had a week's worth of food. And thanks to her *onkel's* extensive kitchen garden, there was still some vegetables before the winter frosts set in.

She tried to put Gretel down, but she started to fuss. "Are you ready for your feeding now?"

Gretel opened her mouth wide and started to howl. Sarah, deciding that qualified as, "Yes," scooped her up and fed her. After that, she would just have time to cook some dinner and tidy the house before her guests arrived.

Just as she began cutting up the vegetables, she looked out the kitchen window to see that Joshua was making his way over to where the buggy had been parked. A minute later, she heard the horse clip-clopping back down the driveway. It was time to fetch his children from school. Sarah knew by the way he cared for his children that there was a soft heart underneath his harsh exterior.

. . .

RIGHT AT SIX O'CLOCK, Sarah heard the chatter of the two children making their way to her front door. She hurried over and opened the door just before they reached it. The two children greeted her excitedly and asked to see the baby. She pointed to Gretel, who was half-asleep, propped up by pillows on the couch, and they ran over to her.

"Mind her. Don't push her over," Joshua called after the children.

"Dinner's nearly ready," Sarah said to Joshua who was still looking anxiously over toward the children. "We can sit for awhile." Sarah walked over to the couch and the two children, who were now kneeling down looking at the baby. They were excited that Gretel was watching them, too.

Once Sarah and Joshua were sitting down, Holly spotted the sewing in the room and she bounded to her feet. "Can I see your sewing, Mrs. Kurtz?"

"*Jah,* of course."

"Don't bother Mrs. Kurtz, Holly," Joshua snapped.

"It's all right. I'm happy to show her." Sarah stood up and gathered her sewing and sat back down. "Sit down beside me here and I'll show you what I'm making." She unfolded the beginnings of a dress she was making for Gretel.

"Do you have a sewing machine?"

"I had one, but I left it behind when I moved. When I was a little girl of your age, I didn't have a machine, so I'm used to doing everything by hand. I don't mind it even though it's a lot slower."

"Can you show me how to sew?"

"Holly, you can't ask something like that."

Sarah smiled when she saw the earnestness in Holly's eyes as she stared up at her. "I'd be happy to teach you to sew as long as it's all right with your *vadder*."

"Could I, *Dat*?"

He frowned.

"I'd love to teach her," Sarah said.

He nodded and gave a small smile.

Holly then whipped her head around to look at Sarah. "Can you show me now?"

Sarah laughed. "I've got the dinner to serve, then we have to eat it, and then we'll have dessert."

"*Jah,* and after that, it'll be your bedtime," Joshua told Holly.

"What about tomorrow after *schul,* Mrs. Kurtz?"

"I think that might be okay. As long as that's all right with your *vadder.*"

"That'll be fine," he said.

"*Gut.* I'll look forward to it."

"Can I help with the *boppli* too while I'm here tomorrow?" Holly asked.

"That would be *wunderbaar.* I'd like some help." It gladdened Sarah's heart to see the happiness beaming from Holly's face. It seemed she missed being around a woman.

"What will I do?" Benjamin whined.

"You and I can do something together," Joshua said.

"What? Chores?"

"Why would you think we'd do chores? As long as you get most of them done before *schul,* we won't spend the whole time doing chores."

"I'll do mine before *schul.* And then I'll go home after sewing in time to help you with dinner, *Dat,*" Holly said.

He chuckled. "Okay."

"I'll just check on the food. It might be ready." Sarah looked at the children. "Would you both mind looking after Gretel so that she doesn't fall?"

"*Jah,*" the children chorused.

She stood up and left her baby on the couch while she hurried to see if everything was ready. When she saw that the meat and vegetables were cooked through, she pulled them out of the oven. It had been a while since she'd had people over for dinner.

The table had already been set and all she had to do was put the bowls in the center of the table.

Sarah put her baby in the crib upstairs, and then they took seats around the table in the kitchen. They said their silent prayers of thanks for the food and then they helped themselves to the food in the center.

"Did you see the new horse?" Sarah asked the children.

"*Jah, Dat* pointed to him in the paddock. We wanted to go and say hello to him, but *Dat* said it wasn't our horse and we should keep away," Benjamin said.

CHAPTER 12

But they that wait upon the LORD shall renew
their strength;
they shall mount up with wings as eagles;
they shall run, and not be weary;
and they shall walk, and not faint.
Isaiah 40:31

SARAH LOOKED over at Joshua wondering
why he was being so strict. What would it
have mattered if the children had patted the

horse? She couldn't go against him and tell his children they could pat him. Besides, he could have had a reason he didn't want them to. When he looked up and met her confused gaze, he looked away.

"You both like horses?"

"*Jah,* we do and *Dat* loves them too. He told me that when he was a boy, he talked about horses all the time and got into trouble from his *vadder* for talking too much."

Joshua gave a little chuckle. "My *vadder* was quite a stern man. It didn't take much for me to get into trouble."

"And what was your *mudder* like? Was she stern too?" Sarah guessed that she was.

"I don't remember her." He popped food into his mouth.

"*Dat's Mamm* died like our *Mamm.*"

"And our other *Dat,*" Holly added.

She looked at Joshua and he glanced at her. There was an awkward silence.

"More bread anyone?" Sarah asked lifting up a plate of sliced bread.

"*Nee denke,*" the children said in turn while Joshua shook his head.

Sarah placed the bread back on the table searching her mind for something to change the subject. "We've got apple pie for dessert."

"That's *Dat's* favorite," Holly said.

"That's right, it is," Benjamin said.

"We should try to cook that soon, *Dat,*" Holly suggested.

"Maybe Mrs. Kurtz will show you how to do it so it doesn't turn out wrong like the last one," Benjamin said.

Sarah giggled at the way Benjamin's lip curled up at the corners. "What happened to it?"

Holly laughed. "It was burned on the edges and the middle was all sunken in."

"Are you telling tales on me, you two?"

"*Nee,* we're just telling the truth like you always tell us," Holly said.

"It sounds like you had the oven on far too hot. You've got to give a pie time to cook evenly throughout, with the oven at a moderate temperature."

"We were in a hurry and wanted to eat it. I guess you're right; we must've had the oven too hot."

The two children giggled.

"This food is really nice, Mrs. Kurtz."

"Denke. I'm glad you like it."

"Dat can't cook at all," Benjamin said.

Joshua frowned. "I'm getting better."

"What kind of food do you cook?" Sarah asked.

Holly got in first before Joshua could answer, "We either have chicken or coleslaw or fish and roast vegetables."

"I can cook other things," Joshua said.

"Who's going to teach me to cook?" Holly asked her *vadder.*

"We've talked about this, Holly. We can both learn together."

"Men don't cook," Benjamin said.

"You just told me your *vadder* does," Sarah said to Benjamin.

"*Jah,* that's what you said, Benjamin." Holly giggled.

"I mean that most men don't cook. Most normal men who are married don't cook because the lady cooks."

"What is the man supposed to do if he has no wife, is he supposed to starve?" Joshua asked his son.

"*Nee,* because then we'd starve." Benjamin gave a cheeky smile.

Joshua lifted his chin up slightly. "We should all learn together."

"I'm not learning," Benjamin said. "If you want to learn, *Dat,* Mrs. Kurtz might teach you and Holly because she cooks good."

"Mrs. Kurtz might have enough to do with teaching Holly stitching."

"You don't say stitching, *Dat.* It's just called sewing."

"Oh, pardon me for getting it wrong."

Holly giggled.

Now that he was here with his children, Sarah was seeing more of the softer side of Joshua, and it was a side that she liked.

"Who wants dessert?" Sarah asked.

"Me!" Holly shot up her hand.

"Me too," Benjamin said.

"Make that three. I'll be in on that too," Joshua said.

AFTER THEY HAD EATEN DESSERT, Joshua said that the children needed to get their sleep. He offered to stay behind and help with the cleanup, but Sarah refused his help.

"Can I say goodnight to Gretel?" Holly said in a tiny voice before they reached the front door.

"Gretel's asleep, Holly," Joshua said.

"If you're very quiet, I can take you up to see her."

"Can I, *Dat?*"

He nodded.

"Me too?" Benjamin asked.

"Okay."

Sarah took one of the lanterns from the living room and walked upstairs with the two children following her. She pushed the door of Gretel's room open and placed the lantern on the dresser.

The two children peeped in the crib.

"*Gut nacht,* Gretel," Holly whispered.

"*Gut nacht,*" Benjamin echoed.

After a moment, Sarah picked up the lantern again and they followed her back down the stairs.

Their father had moved to the couch and he jumped up when he saw them approach. "Was she awake?"

"*Nee,* she was asleep. I hope she's awake when I come here tomorrow," Holly said.

Sarah nodded. "She could be."

Joshua stood in the doorway. *"Denke* for having us to dinner."

"Jah, denke," Benjamin said.

"Denke," Holly said.

"You're all very welcome and *denke* for coming here. I'll see you tomorrow after *schul,* Holly."

"I won't forget. I'll come straight here."

"Gut."

"I'll see you tomorrow morning if you're awake when I bring the eggs," Benjamin said.

"Let's go." Joshua walked out of the door with his children.

Sarah stood in the doorway and watched them until they disappeared around the corner. When there was no more sign of them, she stepped back and closed the door. Just as she was heading to the kitchen to clean up, Gretel started to cry. When she glanced over at the clock, she saw it was already nine o'clock.

CHAPTER 13

And now abideth faith, hope, charity, these
three;
but the greatest of these is charity.
1 Corinthians 13:13

THE NEXT AFTERNOON, Holly knocked on
Sarah's door.

"Hello, Mrs. Kurtz."

"Hello, come inside. Let's sit down on the
couch." Sarah sat down and Holy sat right

next to her. Sarah leaned forward and picked up her sewing. "I'll teach you how to sew on Gretel's dress and then we can sew something else after that."

"Okay. Can I try?"

"You can. I'll show you what to do first."

Sarah showed her the right way to hold the needle and how to hold the fabric, and then demonstrated a few stitches. "Now you have a go."

They stayed sewing for half an hour.

"That might be enough for today. Just push the needle halfway in and leave it there."

Holly did as she was told and handed the sewing back to Sarah. "Very good, Holly, you've done a nice job. All those stitches are so even."

"I just did them the same as yours. Will you get another sewing machine soon?"

"*Jah,* I think I will."

"Can you show me how to use it when you get it?"

"I will. Who sewed your dress?"

Holly looked down at her dress. *"Dat* gets my dresses for me from somewhere, but he didn't say where from. I don't know where he got them. He didn't sew them because he can't sew."

Joshua knocked on the open front door. "Hello, is Holly finished yet?"

Still sitting, Holly said, "Can't I stay longer? I haven't played with Gretel yet."

"She might sleep for longer. Best you go home with your *vadder* and you can see her after *schul* tomorrow."

"Can I, *Dat?*"

"Okay. Come on, you have to get some things done."

"Do you want to see what I did, *Dat?*"

"Jah, come inside and see how well she's sewing already."

Joshua stepped inside and inspected Holly's sewing.

"I did these stitches, all the way from here up to here."

"That's very *gut!*"

"She did a great job. As soon as I showed her, she started sewing as though she'd been doing it forever."

Holly looked pleased with herself as she stood up. "I'll see you tomorrow, Mrs. Kurtz."

"*Gut nacht,* Holly." Sarah smiled and rose to her feet.

"*Denke* for spending the time with Holly like this. It's nice for her to spend some time with a woman."

"We've had a lovely time together."

Holly flung her arms around her waist and Sarah was taken aback. She lightly encircled her arms about her and then the girl stepped back.

Joshua lightly touched Holly on her

shoulders. "Come on. We've taken up enough of Mrs. Kurtz's time."

"See you tomorrow."

"I'll be waiting," Sarah said.

Joshua turned and gave her a big smile before they walked out the door.

Sarah closed the door, pleased that she was able to spend time with Holly.

When Gretel grows up I'll be able to have some lovely times like this with her, she thought.

THE NEXT AFTERNOON when Holly came to the house, Sarah shared an idea.

"Holly, would you like to sew something for your *vadder* and your *bruder* for Christmas?"

Her face lit up. "I'd love that. Would I be a good enough sewer to do that?"

"*Jah,* I'll help you and show you what you need to do."

"When could we start?"

"As soon as we think of what you could make them. Do you have any ideas?"

"Maybe something small. How far away is Christmas?"

"It's only eight weeks away. It'll go quickly."

'What about a shirt for *Dat?*"

"That might be a little too big. I was thinking something more like a sampler with a bible verse that he could put on the wall in his bedroom."

"Okay. What would the bible verse say?"

"How about 'Watch and Pray'? That's what I had in the *haus* where I was growing up. It's simple and uncomplicated and it would mean a lot to your *vadder.*"

"Okay. Can we do it in brown and green? *Dat* is always talking about all the different trees when we're going anywhere, so I know he likes trees and they're green and brown."

"Very good. Green and brown go nicely together."

Holly clapped her hands together. "When can we start?"

"Tomorrow night we're all going to dinner at Nellie's, I mean, Mrs. Yoder's *haus*. What about Friday after *schul,* and then we can continue it whenever you come here? We can hide it here so no one can see it until Christmas. If we do a little bit every time, we will have it finished by Christmas."

"That would be *wunderbaar! Denke,* Mrs. Kurtz. I'm glad you thought of it."

Sarah gave a little giggle. "And for your *bruder,* how about a white handkerchief with dark blue initials?"

"*Jah,* I think he likes blue."

CHAPTER 14

For we are saved by hope:
but hope that is seen is not hope:
for what a man seeth, why doth he yet hope for?
Romans 8:24

DINNER AT THE YODERS' house came around quickly. Besides Joshua and his two children, and Bishop Peter and Mary, there was one older couple there as well as the single man that Mary had told Sarah about. Now they were all sitting in the living room before the dinner was served.

"Can I sit next to, Mrs. Kurtz?" Holly asked Nellie.

"We're having both of you sit at the childrens' table and the adults will sit at the big table."

Sarah looked at Holly and saw her disappointed face. Holly was used to talking with the adults at the dinner table.

When Nellie left the room for the kitchen, Sarah followed her. "Can I help you with anything in here?"

"*Nee,* it's all done here. I'm just waiting. How is everything with your neighbors? You seem to be getting along well with them."

"I am, and I'm teaching Holly to sew."

Nellie swung around. "Joshua is allowing that?"

Sarah giggled. "Of course he is. I'm not teaching her in secret."

"That is a little surprising."

"Why's that?"

"He's always been so protective." She leaned closer, and said in a low voice, "A few of the women have tried to get to him through the *kinner*. They'll offer to do this and that for them or to take them places. He has never accepted their offers."

"*Gut*. He must know that I'm not a scheming woman out to trap him."

Nellie gave her a disapproving look. "These women aren't scheming, Sarah. I've known most of them all my life."

"I didn't really mean that. I just meant that my motivation is different. Besides, it was Holly who asked if I could teach her sewing."

"Well, I'm glad he allowed that. She needs a woman to teach her things."

"I agree. He can't teach her sewing and the like. And from what the children have said, he can't teach Holly to cook either, because he can't cook himself."

The two women giggled.

"Benjamin brings eggs to me every morning and leaves them at my door. If I'm awake, he'll talk for a while. It's nice to have them living there. I don't feel so alone."

"What do you think of the young man out there?"

Sarah peeked around the door at the visitor. "He seems nice, but I don't think he's for me."

"*Jah,* I figured you'd say that. Especially when I saw you arriving with Joshua."

"I wouldn't start thinking anything like that, Nellie."

Nellie raised her eyebrows. "We shall see."

ON SATURDAY AFTERNOON, Sarah was sitting quietly on her couch with her baby asleep in the crib beside her when she heard a dreadful squeal. She wasn't certain whether the squeal was from an animal or from a human. When the squeal persisted, she hurried outside to see where it was coming from.

Under a tree behind the barn, Joshua and Benjamin were leaning over Holly. Sarah ran to them and crouched down beside them. Holly was clutching her arm.

"It must be broken. We'll need to go to the hospital," Benjamin said.

Joshua looked closely at Holly's hand and arm. "I've had a lot to do with broken bones. She's sprained her wrist. It'll most likely be painful."

"Are you sure? It looks swollen," Benjamin said.

"I'm quite sure." He lifted Holly into his arms. "She needs rest and we need ice on it."

"I've got ice," Sarah said.

"Good, because we don't have any."

"I'll go and get it now." While Sarah ran to get ice, Joshua carried Holly back to his house.

When Sarah ran inside, she looked over to see her baby still fast asleep. She broke up the large block of ice with an icepick and hurried back to the *grossdaddi haus* with a bowl of ice chips.

Holly was lying on the couch sobbing and Joshua was unwinding a roll of bandage.

She passed him the bowl.

"Denke."

"What can I do?" Sarah asked.

"That's fine. We're okay now *denke.*"

"Nee, stay, Mrs. Kurtz. Sit by me. I don't want you to go."

Joshua stopped what he was doing and stared at her.

"I can stay a few minutes, but I have Gretel asleep next door."

"Denke," Holly whimpered.

Joshua folded some ice into one of the

bandages and carefully wrapped it around Holly's arm while Benjamin looked on.

"What were you doing?" Joshua barked at Benjamin.

"We were climbing a tree."

"I know that, but why?"

"It's fun. We do it all the time and she's never fallen before."

Joshua shook his head.

"It's not my brother's fault, *Dat.* It was just an accident."

"This will stop your sewing," Joshua said, which made Holly cry.

"I think it'll be okay. We can manage. The main work is done with the right hand and the fabric is held still with the left. I think we can work around it until it heals."

Then Sarah heard Gretel cry. "I'll have to go and feed Gretel."

"*Nee,* please stay. Can you bring her back here?" Holly asked.

Sarah glanced at Joshua who gave a nod.

"I'll feed her and come back with her."

"Please hurry." Holly's voice was now a small whine.

"I will."

CHAPTER 15

Better are the wounds of a friend,
than the deceitful kisses of an enemy.
Proverbs 27:6

SARAH FED GRETEL and then took her along to see Holly, who was still lying on the couch with her wrist wrapped in the iced bandage.

"I was as quick as I could be. And I've brought some arnica oil. It's a special blend that I keep on hand. We can rub it on her arm when it's done being iced."

"*Gut!* I've heard of that. It reduces swelling?"

"*Jah,* and bruising; it does all kinds of good things."

"Sit by me?" Holly asked Sarah.

Sarah sat down and placed the small bottle of oil on the table while balancing Gretel in her other arm.

"Would you like me to take Gretel?" Joshua asked.

"Okay."

Joshua reached down and took Gretel out of her arms. Holly took hold of Sarah's hand and clutched it tightly before she closed her eyes.

"Will she be okay?" Benjamin asked Sarah.

"She'll be fine. It might hurt for a few days and be a little uncomfortable."

"No climbing trees again," Joshua said.

"Okay. Did you climb trees when you were a girl, Mrs. Kurtz?" Benjamin asked.

"Maybe once or twice when I was visiting friends. I didn't have any siblings, so I mostly helped my *mudder* with the work around the *haus* and with the cooking."

"And sewing?" Holly asked, her eyes still closed.

"*Jah*, and the sewing." Sarah looked over to see Joshua walking around patting her baby on her back. "She looks quite comfortable with you."

"She's not crying, so that's a start."

"*Dat* loves *bopplis*," Holly opened her eyes and lifted her head to watch him.

"Does he?"

"*Jah*, he does."

"Who doesn't?" Joshua said.

"They're more fun when they're bigger and can laugh and play. How old will Gretel be when she can walk?" Benjamin asked.

"Most likely when she's around one year

old. Some babies walk before then, but some don't walk until closer to two years. They're all different."

"If you want to put her down, Benjamin might go and bring the crib in from next door. It's pretty small."

"*Jah,* would you do that, Benjamin?" Joshua asked.

"Okay. Where is it?"

"It's in the living room."

When Benjamin left to get the crib, Joshua said, "I could hold her all day, but I do have to get the evening meal on."

"I could do that for you," Sarah offered

"*Nee,*" Holly squealed, holding her hand tighter. "Stay by me, please. You make me feel better."

"You stay there. I'll start cooking when Benjamin brings the crib back. After dinner, Holly, I'll bandage your wrist and you must keep it raised. You can sleep on the couch tonight."

"Okay," Holly whimpered.

"You'll stay for dinner, Mrs. Kurtz."

"Nee, I'll be fine."

"I'm telling you, you'll stay for dinner. You wouldn't be able to get a meal cooked while you're sitting here with us."

"Okay, *denke."*

"Dat's bossy," Holly whispered.

"What's that, Holly?" Joshua asked.

"I said you're bossy."

"Holly! If you weren't injured, I'd have you go to your room for that. You don't disrespect adults."

Sarah tried not to look at Holly through fear of Holly seeing she was amused. He was indeed bossy and now she knew she wasn't the only one who had noticed. Joshua was bossy and controlling, but it was always for the best reasons, from what she could tell.

When Benjamin brought the crib back, Joshua instructed him to place it close to Sarah and then Joshua lay Gretel into it.

"Now, I'll start on the food. Benjamin, you can come and help me."

"What?"

"No arguments. The women are doing other things right now."

Sarah sat there beside Holly who had her eyes closed, but Sarah knew she wasn't asleep because she still had a tight grip on her hand.

When the dinner was ready, Holly still insisted that Sarah stay by her. Sarah sat and ate her food and helped Holly eat hers.

"*Denke* for helping us today, Sarah," Joshua said as he took up both dinner plates.

"I'm happy to help. Shall we put that arnica oil on her now?"

"I want you to do it, Mrs. Kurtz." Holly pouted.

"How about I massage the oil on and then your *vadder* can bandage it after that?"

"Okay. It won't hurt will it?"

"*Nee,* it won't. I'll just massage it in

slightly with my fingertips." Sarah looked around. "I'll need a towel to get all the moisture off her arm."

"I'll get one." Benjamin hurried to get a towel.

Sarah could hear Joshua in the kitchen washing the dishes.

"Here you are." Benjamin handed her a white towel.

Sarah wiped Holly's hand carefully and then rubbed a generous amount of oil all over her hand, wrist and up her arm. "That's not hurting is it?'

"It doesn't hurt when it's still, but does a little when it's moved."

She continued to massage the oil until Joshua returned from the kitchen. "Okay, now your *vadder* will wrap it in a bandage."

Sarah stood up.

"*Nee,* Mrs. Kurtz, please stay sitting by me."

"Holly, Mrs. Kurtz has to go home."

"Please stay here tonight?"

"She can't."

Holly started sobbing and the sobs turned into howls. Joshua and Sarah looked at each other.

Sarah whispered, "I could perhaps stay tonight if we move the other couch over here, next to her. That is, if you don't mind?"

He nodded. "What about the *boppli?*"

"She's been sleeping through the night, so I won't have to feed her until early morning and she almost certainly won't wake again before then." Sarah looked into the crib where her baby was sleeping soundly.

"Are you certain? I don't know how comfortable the couch will be."

"It'll be fine. I don't mind at all."

"You'll stay?" Holly asked.

"*Jah,* your *Dat* said it was okay. We'll move the couch and I can stay by you all night."

"Will you hold my hand?"

"*Jah*, I'll hold your hand."

Holly smiled and wiped her eyes.

Her father leaned down and kissed his daughter on her forehead. "You see? There's no need to cry, but it's only this once. Mrs. Kurtz has her own home to sleep at. It's just this once."

"Okay."

Benjamin helped his father move the couch.

"Do you have enough blankets? I could get some from my *haus*."

"*Nee*, we have plenty of pillows and blankets."

Holly smiled and Sarah settled down with her. Minutes later, Joshua brought her two pillows and two blankets.

After Benjamin went to bed, Joshua sat there in the lounge.

CHAPTER 16

He that loveth not knoweth not God;
for God is love.
1 John 4:8

"DENKE FOR DOING THIS, Sarah. Not many women would go to this much trouble."

Sarah glanced at Holly who was now sleeping. "I think many women would do this for you and your *kinner.*"

"I know I haven't been an easy man to get along with. I've had a few struggles."

"We've all had struggles."

"I suppose you've heard that Benjamin and Holly are the *kinner* of my late *fraa?* Other than from them recently?"

"Jah, I heard that. She was a widow when you met and she died soon after."

"That's right. I grew up an only child to one parent. My mother became a widow at a young age. I watched the struggles she went through to give me a *gut* life. I didn't realize how hard things would've been for her until I got older. When I met Katherine, who was recently widowed, I didn't want her to struggle like my *mudder* had to. We got married fairly quickly."

Sarah stared into his eyes, wondering why he was telling her all this. And she had to wonder whether he had really been in love with his *fraa,* or whether he married her to help her.

"I grew up as an only child as well. I don't want Gretel to be alone, like I was always alone. I was surrounded by adults and I always wanted many *kinner*. Now it looks like it might just be me and Gretel."

"You'll marry again, if that's what you want."

"You think so?"

He smiled and gave a nod.

"I liked being married. It was nice to have someone to do things for and always having someone there. I even like having you living next door rather than living here all on my own."

"You like having people around?" he asked.

"I do. I don't like being alone."

"I think I'm alright on my own, but I'm grateful to have Benjamin and Holly. They're everything to me."

"*Jah,* I couldn't imagine being without

Gretel. She's the only thing that kept me going after Joel died."

"He died recently?"

"*Jah*. He knew that we were having a *boppli*. He was out of work and he was traveling to get a job with his cousin. It meant that he would work two months away and have one week at home. It wasn't ideal, but that was the only work he could get. He died on the bus coming home. There was a bad accident and five people died, and he was one of them."

"I'm sorry to hear that."

Sarah wiped away a tear. "Most of the time I try not to think about him. It's easier that way."

"I thought I would never marry again, but seeing how Holly is with you makes me think that she needs a *mudder*."

Sarah wondered whether he thought that she might make a good wife for him and then it would solve all their problems. A marriage to Joshua would make sense. They could blend their families and in time have more children.

Sarah said, "I think all children need both a *mudder* and a *vadder*."

He was silent and she wondered what he was thinking.

"I might stretch my legs now that Holly is asleep."

"The bathroom is off from the kitchen."

"*Denke.* I might get myself a glass of water."

"Would you like a cup of tea, or something?"

"*Nee, denke.* I'll be okay with just the water."

After Sarah had gone to the bathroom, she was in the kitchen drinking water when Holly woke up.

"Where's Mrs. Kurtz?"

"She's in the kitchen," Joshua answered in a calming tone.

"Is she coming back?"

"*Jah,* close your eyes. She said she'd stay here tonight."

"Do you mean it?"

"Of course I do."

Sarah drank her water quickly and hurried back to Holly. "I'm here. I was just having a glass of water. Do you want anything?"

"*Nee, denke.* Will you hold my hand again?"

"Okay. Your *vadder* has moved the couch close to you so I can lie down too."

Holly gradually closed her eyes but not before reaching out her hand.

Sarah took hold of her hand and got comfortable.

"I'll leave you both to it. Call out if you need anything, Sarah. I really appreciate you doing this."

"I'm happy to do it."

"I'll leave the low light burning in the corner."

"Denke."

CHAPTER 17

Greater love hath no man than this,
that a man lay down his life for his friends.
John 15:3

JOSHUA AND SARAH WOKE EARLY, before the children.

Sarah opened her eyes and sat up when she saw Joshua come into the room. Sarah had slept fully clothed.

Joshua sat down beside her. "I'm sorry I

unburdened myself on you last night and told you all my problems."

Sarah shook her head. "You hardly did that. And I did a little unburdening myself."

Holly opened her eyes and looked around. "You're still here?"

"I told you I'd stay by you all night. Before Gretel wakes, I'd like to take another look at your wrist."

Her father helped her sit up. Holly held out her wrist while Sarah carefully unwrapped the bandages.

"It still hurts," Holly said.

"You can stay home from *schul* today."

"*Nee,* I want to go, *Dat.*"

He chuckled. "You can go if you wish."

"Could you fetch me the oil?" Sarah asked Joshua.

He looked around and came back from the kitchen with it in his hands. Sarah rubbed the oil into Holly's wrist and then bandaged it again.

"The swelling's gone down."

"*Gut!*" Joshua said.

"I'll wake up Benjamin to collect those eggs and I'll make everyone some breakfast."

"I must get home. I'd like to get home before Gretel wakes. Would you help me with the crib?"

Joshua nodded.

"*Denke* for staying with me all night," Holly said.

Sarah leaned forward and kissed Holly on her forehead. Then Sarah stood up, and Joshua helped her carry Gretel back next door.

THE NEXT TIME Sarah saw Joshua was after he'd taken the children to school. He knocked on her door.

Sarah was a little surprised to see him there. "Would you care for a cup of *kaffe?* Gretel's asleep and I have a little time."

"Denke, I'd like that." He stepped into the house.

"Come through to the kitchen and I'll put the pot on to boil."

After she put the pot on the stove, she sat down with him at the kitchen table. "How's Holly feeling?"

"She's fine. I told her she could stay home, but she wanted to go to *schul.* I said she has to keep her wrist still."

"Jah, I was there when she said she wanted to go to *schul.* I'm surprised. I thought she'd want a day or two off."

"She might as well be there."

"I suppose so, but she could lie down at home and rest."

"I agree, but she felt she was alright. It must have been the arnica you massaged in last night and this morning."

"It does work wonderfully well."

"I'll have to get some."

"I can give you some. I make my own

mixture."

He nodded and Sarah thought he didn't look too interested in having some of her arnica oil. Perhaps he had come to propose and suggest they merge their families? It certainly would make sense; it was a practical idea. And what's more, she knew Benjamin and Holly liked her as much as she liked them.

"The water's boiling."

"Oh." She jumped up and proceeded to make the coffee. "Would you like a cookie with it?"

"*Nee denke*. I've only just had breakfast."

Sarah placed a mug in front of him and then sat down again.

"Sarah, the reason I came over here is that I was hoping to discuss something very important with you."

"What is it?"

"It hasn't been easy raising the children on my own. They only have me and it doesn't help when they grow an attachment to someone else."

Something wasn't right. This did not sound like the proposal that Sarah had wanted to hear. "I'm not certain of what you're trying to say."

He took a sip of coffee and then placed the mug back on the table. "It's like this. You're not always going to be around. We'll be gone from here in a few months and then we'll be on our own again. I don't want Holly getting used to having a woman around."

Sarah frowned. "Aren't you considering getting married again at some stage?"

"Some people aren't meant for marriage."

"Weren't you happy when you were married?"

"The marriage was too brief to tell. From what I've heard, everyone is happy at the beginning of a marriage and unfortunately Katherine and I only had the beginning—the happy part."

"So, do you want me to keep away from the children?"

"*Jah.*"

Sarah scowled at him. "You can't mean that."

"I do. It's the only thing that makes sense."

Sarah pressed her lips firmly together. Now she was glad that he didn't propose to her. The two of them were miles apart in their thinking. "That'll be a hard thing to do. Benjamin brings me eggs in the morning and Holly and I have sewing projects that we've planned. You can't do that to me. I've come to… enjoy having them around."

He took a mouthful of coffee. "That's the way it has to be."

"I'm not happy about it. Are you sure you have to do things this way? I don't see how that will benefit them. Don't you think they need a woman around?"

"She's growing too attached to you. I know she misses her *mudder,* but Katherine is gone and not coming back. Holly has to face that and grow up."

"She's only a little girl who has lost her father and her mother. It's a blessing that she has you, and I don't mind helping with what she needs. I love having her around and teaching her sewing."

"I can see that you were an only child the way you're so stubborn and want everything your own way. I'm trying to tell you how I want things for my children and you are arguing with me. I tell you, I know what's best for my own *kinner*. I know they weren't born mine, but they're mine now."

"Okay. I'll do as you say and stay away from them. Are you going to tell Holly that she can't come here after *schul* and learn sewing?"

He rubbed his chin and looked as though he hadn't thought about actually telling Holly she couldn't learn sewing any longer.

"Couldn't you just wait until her arm gets

better? If she's feeling better, she won't want me to stay there tonight. I'm not trying to take her *mudder's* place."

"I've got nothing against you. I'm trying to help guard them against more hurt. They've lost one *mudder* in their life and I don't want them to lose another woman they grow close to. You said last night that you're open to marrying again. My thoughts were that if you marry, you'll have no time for them."

How could he be so irritating? So blind? She had been giving him the hint she was open to the idea of marrying him. "I'd never turn my back on them."

"You might not have a choice. If you marry and have more *kinner,* you'll be busy and my *kinner* won't be a priority and that's only natural."

"I'll abide by what you say."

"Maybe you're right. We'll just wait until she gets better and then..."

"Gut. She's excited about sewing and I'd like to teach her some more."

He looked down at his coffee and took another mouthful. "That's all I had to say." He stood up.

She stood up as well and walked him to the door. When he was about to step down the stairs of the porch, he turned and gave a little nod. She nodded back and then closed the door.

Sarah had managed to talk him out of keeping the children away from her. All she could do was slump into the couch, angry with him for being so unreasonable. Hadn't it occurred to him that they could marry and his problems would be solved? Suddenly, a pang went through her heart. She wasn't the kind of woman he wanted to marry and that's why he hadn't thought of them marrying. Any other Amish man would've found marriage a reasonable solution.

Somewhere upstairs, Sarah had a hand

mirror. She sprang to her feet and hurried up the stairs to find it, in amongst the boxes in one of the spare rooms. When she found it, she polished it on her apron and stared into it. Under her eyes were shadows, but she hadn't had much sleep on the couch last night. By no means was she ugly, but she also knew she was no beauty.

Joshua would've found the younger women more attractive and two of them, in particular, had made their interest in him known. The mirror would go back into the box. If Joshua had overlooked her, he wasn't meant to be a husband for her and a father for Gretel. It would've been a solution for both of them, but apparently, it wasn't to be. Tossing the mirror back into the box, Sarah buried her feelings of rejection.

Just when she had started to like him, he showed himself to be unreasonable—again.

CHAPTER 18

He delivereth me from mine enemies:
yea, thou liftest me up above those that rise up
against me:
thou hast delivered me from the violent man.
Psalm 18: 48

DAYS PASSED, and Joshua and she had managed to keep their distance. Holly had still come nearly every day to learn how to sew.

The next Saturday, Joshua knocked on her door and Sarah opened it and saw him alone. "Uh, hello. Where are the children?"

"Off playing somewhere."

"Nowhere near trees I hope."

"*Nee.* She said she'd never climb them again."

"*Gut.*"

"Mind if I come in?"

She stepped aside to allow him through the door. "Have a seat in the living room."

She decided against offering him a cup of coffee as that might lengthen his stay.

"Have you come to talk about Holly?"

"*Nee.* I'm concerned that you and I have become a little strained. We don't talk as we used to."

"I don't know that we ever talked as friends do."

"And that is all my fault. I'm certain of that."

Sarah stared at him wondering what to say.

He continued, "Christmas is approaching and I try to make every Christmas good for my *kinner*. They lost their *mudder* during the holidays, so I try to keep their minds off sorrowful things."

"I didn't know that. Holly never talks much about her *mudder*. I think Christmas is a time when we all think of people who aren't with us anymore. This will be my first Christmas without Joel, and my first one with Gretel."

"They don't talk much about their *mudder,* but I know she's always on their minds."

Sarah was a little annoyed that he didn't comment on what she said. He was only concerned with himself and his children. She pushed a little further to see if he would comment. "I'll miss my husband very much on Christmas day. He would've loved to have just one Christmas with Gretel."

"Sometimes I wonder just how much they miss her. They never talk about her much."

"Joshua, do you ever listen to anything I say, or are you just thinking of the next thing you are about to say?"

He pinched his eyebrows together. "I'm sorry."

"Normally, when people talk there is give and take. You talk about something then I comment and then I might add some comment of my own. I've just shared something personal and you went right on talking about your own things. You really are one of the strangest people I've ever met."

"I don't mean to be like that. I'm sorry. I talk to so few people and when I do I just want to get everything out of me. You're right. I'm selfish. Please tell me something about yourself and I'll listen."

She was tempted to tell him it didn't work like that, but she feared it would be too hard to explain to him exactly how it did work. "Since my husband died, everything has happened so fast. I've had Gretel and then I've moved and now everything is different. I feel... I don't know how I feel. Christmas was a special time for us and now he's not going to be with me." Sarah stared at him. "I'm wondering how I can cope with that. Not only that, I was raised an only child and I don't want that for Gretel, but that means I'll have to marry again, and if I marry a widower with *kinner,* how will he feel about a child who's not his own? I don't want him to favor his own over Gretel. Will that happen?"

Joshua opened his mouth to speak, but Sarah continued, "Then I saw how you are with your *kinner* and they aren't your biological children."

"I love them the same as though they were my own."

"I see that. I see the love you have for

them and that gives me hope that one day Gretel will have a *vadder* who loves her."

He nodded. "You'll find someone."

"Where will I find that man? Will you ever marry?"

"We talked about this the other night. I'm past that time of life, but I often wonder if it would be best for Holly and Benjamin. When I see them with you, I think it would be a good thing for them."

"But not for you?"

He shook his head. "It's hard to say what's good for me. I suppose I should start looking for a suitable *fraa.* But then again, doubts creep in. It's a huge step."

Sarah looked at the cushion beside her and wanted to throw it at him. What was wrong with her? She was around his age and she would be able to see past his rudeness because she'd learned he had a soft and a good heart.

Finally, she had to know. "What about me?"

"You'll find someone in no time at all."

She swallowed her embarrassment for the sake of the three children whose lives would benefit from the match. *"Nee.* What about me and you?"

His eyes opened wide. "I never thought about that."

"Why not?"

He was silent for a while. "I didn't think you'd be interested in a man like me. We never agree on much."

She nodded. "Maybe you spend too much time in your own head, thinking about things when you should be listening."

"Jah, you're probably right. How's the horse working out for you?"

He was changing the subject, but it didn't matter. At least she knew now that he wasn't the slightest bit interested in her. "He was a good choice. He's *wunderbaar."*

"*Gut!* I should leave; I don't want to take up all of your time. Oh, there's just one more thing. The children and I will be visiting tomorrow after the meeting, so it's best we go in separate buggies."

"That's fine. It'll do my horse good to have some exercise."

After she'd walked him to the door, she flopped down on the couch. Never had she felt so rejected. When she was younger, all the men had been flocking around her. Had the years done terrible things to her, or was Joshua irritated with her most of the time just the same as she was irritated by him? No matter which was the reason, or whether there was some other, embarrassment now burned her cheeks. She'd thrown herself at the man, and she'd been brushed aside with equal boldness.

Sarah walked upstairs and peered into the crib. Gretel was just waking up. "Hello. That was good timing. You stayed asleep, allowing your *mamm* to make a huge fool of herself with our neighbor. Now he doesn't want to take us to the Sunday meeting like he normally would."

Just as she leaned down to pick up her daughter, Gretel's bottom lip quivered and she started crying.

"That's exactly how I feel, Gretel, but you'll feel better with a clean diaper and a full tummy. For me, it'll take time. I have to see Joshua every day until he moves out sometime in the new year." She placed Gretel against her shoulder and patted her on her back as she walked to the table for a diaper change.

CHAPTER 19

O Lord, thou hast brought up my soul from the grave:
thou hast kept me alive, that I should not go down to the pit.
Psalm 30:3

SARAH HITCHED the buggy early the next morning, doing her best to avoid Joshua.

Just as she was walking back to the house to fetch Gretel, his children ran over to her.

"Aren't you coming with us this morning?"

"*Nee.* Not today. Gretel and I are going by ourselves."

"Why?"

"You're visiting someone after the meeting and I'm just coming straight home."

"He didn't tell us that," Benjamin said.

"*Vadders* are like that sometimes. He's got a lot on his mind."

"Can I drive there with you?" Holly asked.

"Me too?" Benjamin added.

"Um, I'm not sure."

"Well, is it okay with you if it's okay with *Dat?*"

"I think you should go with your *vadder.*"

"Really?" Benjamin asked.

"Stop bothering Mrs. Kurtz," Joshua called out.

The children walked over to him dragging their feet. Sarah hated to say no to them, but Joshua had already made it clear that he didn't want them getting too close to her. Sarah continued walking to the house to get her baby. Things were getting more awkward because she didn't want to upset Joshua's children.

As soon as she secured Gretel in the buggy, she climbed into the driver's seat and clicked Midnight forward. When she was halfway down the driveway, she looked around to see if the children were still outside the house. They were standing there looking after her as Joshua was saying something to them. She hoped she'd done the right thing; Sarah was certain that Joshua wouldn't have wanted them to travel to the meeting with her.

NOT LONG AFTER Sarah had sat down in the house where the meeting was being held, Holly ran over to her.

"*Dat* says I can sit next to you if it's all

right with you and you aren't already sitting next to anyone."

Sarah smiled. "I'd love to have you sit next to me." Sarah looked up at Joshua who gave her a polite smile, and Benjamin waved when he caught her eye. The men had to sit on one side and the women on the other. That meant that Holly couldn't sit with her brother and father.

"Are you coming for more sewing after *schul* tomorrow?"

"*Jah.* That's what I look forward to when I'm at *schul.*"

"I hope you're listening, too. It's important to learn all you can while you're there."

"I already know it all."

"Do you?"

Holly gave a cheeky smile and nodded.

"So you're a big 'know it all'?"

Holly giggled. "*Jah.*"

"People like you are so annoying."

Holly giggled again. "Ask me anything and I'll tell you the answer."

"Okay. How big is the world?"

"Bigger than infinity."

"Oh, you do know everything."

"Ask me another."

"Why is the sky blue?" Sarah asked.

"Because that's *Gott's* favorite color."

Sarah frowned. "That's not fair. How do I know if that's right or wrong?"

"I told you I know everything. That's why *schul* is a waste of time for me."

"I'm not so sure about that."

When the bishop stood up to say a prayer, a hush of silence swept over the room.

Holly and Sarah closed their eyes. Gretel was asleep and Sarah hoped that she'd stay that way right through the meeting.

Throughout the sermon, Sarah glanced at Joshua several times. It surprised her that he'd allowed Holly to sit with her since they already spent many hours sewing together.

AFTER THE MEETING, Holly ran over to some young friends. There were a few people Sarah wanted to speak with, and then she'd go home.

The meeting was at Seth and Nellie Yoder's house and everyone was cramped inside their home for the meal afterward. It was too cold to go outside in the yard, as they would've in the warmer months. In spite of her better judgment, Sarah found herself looking around to see where Joshua was. She caught sight of him talking to a young woman who was laughing at something he said. Sarah frowned trying to remember when he'd ever said anything remotely funny. This woman was a different one from the two women she'd seen him with before.

Spotting those other two women waiting nearby to talk with Joshua, she knew she had no chance. From their conversations, he wanted a woman who'd be clearly focused on his children and that had to mean a woman who had never married before and had no children.

The best thing Sarah could do, she decided, was to put him out of her mind and concentrate on building a life for herself. That meant getting better acquainted with everyone in the community. What she needed to do was to throw herself into all the activities a woman with a young baby could do.

After volunteering with Maggie Fuller to help with the pie drive, she headed to her buggy with Gretel in her arms.

"Wait, Sarah."

She swung around surprised to see Joshua.

"I need to apologize about this morning. My *kinner* keep bothering you and…"

"Mr. Byler, they're no bother to me. They're anything but a bother, and I didn't like making them feel that they were. I was happy to have them go in my buggy this morning, but I knew you don't like me getting close to them, so I had to make out I wasn't keen on the idea. It felt horrible!"

"I'm trying to find my way, and doing what's the best for them. I've had a lot going on."

"Do you think you're the only one with a lot going on? The only one who's had a loved one die, the only one who worries about raising their *kinner* alone?" She shook her head at him, turned from him and placed Gretel in the basket securely in the buggy. Then she headed to the driver's side.

"Can you stop and listen a moment?"

"*Nee.* I'm done with listening to you. Listening is something that you should try for a change." She walked past him and climbed into the buggy.

He walked up and grabbed the horse's cheek strap so she couldn't leave. "Don't be like this, Sarah. I'm trying to speak with you."

"There's nothing that I want to speak with you about, so kindly let go of my horse."

"Sarah!"

"You always speak down to me. I'm not a child and I'm not a person that you can boss around. I appreciate the things you've helped me with and you've already told me you don't want me to get any closer with your *kinner.* When you leave my *grossdaddi haus,* you won't have me as a problem any longer."

"You've got the wrong idea."

"*Nee,* I have the right idea. I'm only sorry I opened up to you and told you what was on my heart. *That* was when I had the wrong idea."

"You misunderstand me."

Now her anger was rising. "Let go of my horse now or I shall scream."

He pinched his eyebrows together staring at her. Then he let go of the horse and stepped aside.

As she drove away, she resisted the urge to look back and see what he was doing. The best thing she could do was put him out of her mind for good, or try to since he lived next door.

It was times like these that she wished she had her good friend, Matilda, to sit down and talk with. Matilda would've given her good advice. Talking over the phone wasn't as good as talking in person and the barn wasn't the best place to have a long conversation.

WHEN JOSHUA CAME BACK from taking the children to *schul* on Monday morning, he knocked on her door.

Feeling uncomfortable, and too tired from lack of sleep to have another argument, Sarah opened her door.

"Can I come in?"

Sarah stepped aside without saying anything and Joshua made his way to the couch.

"Mind if I sit?" he asked quietly.

"Nee, I don't mind; have a seat."

When they were both seated, he said, "I've come to apologize. I know you're fond of my *kinner* and they're very fond of you. I don't think I should let my fear ruin the friendship that has developed between the three of you."

Sarah breathed out heavily. "Well, I'm glad to hear that."

"Am I forgiven?"

She nodded. *"Jah."*

"Forgiven enough to have a cup of *kaffe?"*

"Don't you have your own hot water at the *grossdaddi haus?"*

He gave an embarrassed laugh. "I've been awful to you."

"As long as that's in the past, I think we can have a cup of *kaffe.*"

"It's in the past."

"*Gut!* Come into the kitchen with me."

When he sat down, she filled the pot with water.

"I do have a rather large favor to ask you. The timing isn't great, since we're mending fences, but…"

"What is it?"

"It's not for a week or so. I was wondering if you might be able to watch the children overnight. Have them here at your *haus?*"

"I don't mind at all. Where are you going? Oh, I'm sorry, you don't have to answer that."

"It's okay. It's no secret. Well, it's a secret to Benjamin and Holly. I'm not sure what I'm going to tell them. I'm collecting Christmas presents for them from my cousin's place, and it's half a day's journey away."

"So, you'll need to stay overnight?"

"Jah."

"I'll always watch them for you. It's no trouble."

He smiled. *"Gut.* I was afraid to ask since we haven't always gotten along well."

"Would you prefer *kaffe* or tea?"

"I'll have some tea for a change."

She poured each of them a cup of tea and then sat down.

CHAPTER 20

For his anger endureth but a moment;
in his favour is life: weeping may endure for a
night,
but joy cometh in the morning.
Psalm 30:5

JOSHUA HADN'T COME HOME when he'd said, and Sarah became worried. She hitched up the buggy to her new horse and took the children to visit Nellie and Seth.

"He's not come home yet?" asked Nellie.

"Nee. I just hope something awful hasn't happened to him," Sarah whispered so the children wouldn't hear. "I was just passing Abram Miller on the way here and he said that he last saw him two days ago in the early morning."

"Jah," said Seth, "Joshua told me he was loaning his buggy to Joseph for two days while he was away."

"Joseph told me that Abram had wanted some help on his barn," said Sarah. She looked confused. "Who's Abram?"

"Abram Miller. Joshua said he'd help Joseph on Abram's old barn when he came back."

Sarah frowned. "That's the last anyone heard of him? Where's Abram's barn?"

"It's the farm next door to Jenny's *haus* where we had the meeting two Sundays ago. The barn is way over to the back of the property."

"Perhaps I should go take a look around."

"There's no point in doing that."

"I need to do something. Would you watch the children while I go?"

"Okay, but do you think you should? It'll be a waste of time."

"I want to, if you don't mind watching them until I get back."

"Sure. They'll be fine. Drive up the driveway and continue past the *haus* in a straight line. Then you'll have to get out and go on foot, but the barn will come into view by then.

"Denke." Sarah told the children she was going out for a while and they would stay with Nellie, along with Gretel.

After she had pulled on her cape, she hurried out to the buggy. As she climbed up behind Midnight, she was glad that he was good and spritely and that she wasn't using the old horse. Although Joshua was bossy and dominating, he'd had her best interests at heart. Something in the pit of her stomach gnawed at her. She knew he was in trouble. That was the only reason that would keep him away from his children.

SARAH DROVE PAST THE HOUSE, just like Nellie had told her, and then she continued on until the ground was too uneven for the buggy. In the distance was an old barn with half a roof. She tied her horse to a fence post and pulling her shawl tighter around her, she hurried toward the barn.

When she stepped into the old barn, her worst fears were confirmed. There was a body on the floor with the lower half covered by a huge wooden beam. Quickly but carefully, she moved closer, and saw that it was Joshua. She shook him vigorously and he opened his eyes.

"Sarah."

She looked back at the beam that was trapping both of his legs.

"How long have you been here?"

His eyelids flickered closed.

"Joshua!"

"*Jah?*"

She moved to the beam and put both her arms under it and tried to heave it away from him. It didn't budge.

"Benjamin and Holly?"

Rushing back to his head, she took off her shawl and covered him. "They're fine. I haven't told them that no one knew where you were. I told them you had to stay longer."

"*Denke.*"

"I'll go and get help."

"*Nee.* Stay."

"I can't, Joshua. I need to find someone to get you out of here."

"*Nee.*" He reached out his hand and she took hold of it. "Stay! I need... to talk."

"Joshua, this can wait. Let me get help and then we can talk."

"Listen… to me…. I've… thinking." His speech was halted due to his body shivering violently.

"Save your strength."

"Marry… me?"

"What?"

"I've… thought…."

"I need to get help." Sarah sprang to her feet and ran all the way back out to her buggy. She stopped at the nearest house and hoped they had a phone.

When she told the owners what had happened, they ran out to their barn to call for help while Sarah went back to Joshua.

"I'm back. Help's on the way." She wrapped her shawl more snugly around him. "You're cold."

He didn't stop trembling.

"I've thought… you…"

"Don't talk. Save your strength." All she

could do was hold his hand. She didn't know if she should rub his back to keep him warm, as that might have been bad for his circulation that had to have been cut off with the beam on his legs.

Sarah heaved a sigh of relief when she heard the sirens. The paramedics raced in with a stretcher and Sarah jumped to her feet.

"You'll need to get this off him," she called out, pointing to the beam.

"The fire department's on its way, Ma'am," one of the three paramedics replied.

Sarah stepped back and walked out of the barn. The fire department arrived within minutes and went about setting him free while Sarah paced up and down. When they carried him out on a stretcher, she ran over to them. One paramedic was carrying an IV drip high in the air and the other two men had hold of either end of the stretcher.

"How is he?"

"He's in shock and it looks like he's got some broken bones. It's a concern that he's been there in the cold. Just as well he was wearing his heavy coat."

"Do you want to travel to the hospital with your husband?" one of the paramedics asked.

"I've got to get back to the children. Where are you taking him?"

While they answered her, she looked down at his dirt-covered face. His eyes were closed, and then his eyelids slowly opened.

"I'll come and see you soon, Joshua."

His eyelids closed.

Once the ambulance drove away, she got into her buggy and made her way back to the Yoders' *haus*, wondering how she would break the news to his children.

When she arrived back at Nellie's house, Nellie had already been told what was going on by someone from the family who owned the farm that the ambulance was called from.

"We've been waiting to hear how he is."

"He'll be fine. They were taking him to the hospital."

"Can we see him?" Benjamin asked, looking at her with wide eyes.

"Jah, we'll all go and see him."

"I'll stay and mind the *boppli* if you want to take Benjamin and Holly with you. I'll take Gretel back to your *haus* and make her a bottle."

"Would you?"

"Jah. If you want to head off to the hospital now, the best way is by taxi."

"Denke, Nellie. I'll call one now." Sarah hurried to Nellie's barn to call a taxi, glad that she'd introduced the baby to the bottle and now was only giving her nightly breastfeeds.

AT THE HOSPITAL, they were shown to a waiting room. When a doctor finally came out, he informed them that Joshua had suffered a mild concussion in addition to other injuries, and he told them he was lucky to be alive.

"We had to cut him out of his clothes. He'd managed to push his hands under his coat and that helped him avoid frostbite. If he hadn't had so many layers of clothing on, the outcome wouldn't have been good, with him being trapped on the ground like that."

"Does he have broken bones?"

"He has a broken leg."

"Put some arnica oil on it, like you did for me," Holly said to Sarah.

"It'll take more than that for a broken leg, Holly."

"*Jah,* it'll have to be strapped still," Benjamin said to his sister.

Sarah asked, "Will he be okay?"

"He'll be okay, but he'll need to stay here under observation for a few days and then he'll be allowed home. You can see him now, but he's sleeping. We gave him something for the pain, which would've made him drowsy. His feet and hands were in the early stages of frostbite, but he won't suffer any permanent damage."

"Good. Thank you, Doctor. Can we see him now?"

"Come this way. He's still in emergency and very sleepy. We're still treating his frostbite, but he'll be taken to a room as soon as one becomes available."

"How long will that take?" Sarah asked.

"Not too long."

She looked at the children who were walking by her side. "Remember what the doctor said, he won't be able to talk much. We'll have a quick visit now and then we'll come back and see him tomorrow."

"Okay," Benjamin said while Holly nodded solemnly.

They were taken into a section of the emergency department where people were in beds separated one from another by curtains. The doctor led them to the end where two men were doing something with Joshua's legs.

"*Dat,*" Holly said quietly.

He opened his eyes.

Sarah leaned down and suggested to Benjamin that he take his sister over closer. "Tell him we'll be back tomorrow and we'll pray for his fast recovery."

Benjamin nodded and then led his sister by the hand closer to their father's bedside.

After they had been there for a few moments, Sarah walked up behind them. "We'll go now, Joshua."

He gave the tiniest of nods, and slowly closed his eyes.

"Bye, *Dat.*"

"Bye," Benjamin said.

Slowly his eyes opened, blinked once, and then they closed.

"Come along. He needs to sleep."

She guided them out of the area and back through the front doors of the hospital, looking for the taxi stand.

THAT NIGHT when Joshua's children were asleep in the bedroom beside hers, and Gretel was asleep in her crib, Sarah slipped into bed exhausted. She closed her eyes and said another prayer of thanks for Joshua being found in time in the broken down old barn. Nellie had told her she'd heard that Joshua had run into someone who had asked him to take a look and decide if his barn could be repaired or if it'd be better knocked down, and that was why Joshua had been in the barn. When the man didn't hear back from Joshua, he had just assumed that he hadn't yet gotten to the barn.

CHAPTER 21

Thou hast turned for me my mourning into
dancing:
thou hast put off my sackcloth,
and girded me with gladness;
Psalm 30:11

THE NEXT DAY, Sarah left Gretel with Nellie
again and took Joshua's children back to the
hospital to see him. The front desk gave
them the number of his room, and when

they walked in they saw him sitting up in bed.

He smiled when the children ran over to him, and he held out his arms. They threw their arms around him.

"Are you better, *Dat?*" Benjamin asked.

"Much better. I'm fine. A little bit sore and sorry, but I'm fine." He looked over at Sarah.

"When are you coming home?" Holly asked.

"Soon I hope. Sarah, *denke* for bringing them here; I hope they haven't been too much trouble."

"*Nee.* They've been a *gut* help to me." She held up a small bag. "I've got some things in here for you, and some spare clothes."

"*Denke.* I appreciate that."

"Have you got broken bones, *Dat?*" Holly asked.

"It seems I have a broken leg, but I'll be able to get around on crutches. I've already seen the physical therapist this morning and tomorrow he'll show me how to use the crutches. Where's Gretel?"

"Nellie is looking after her."

"*Gut.* But I'd have liked to hold her again."

When Sarah heard someone else come into the room behind her, she turned to see two young women—the ones who were always talking to Joshua—Elizabeth and Sadie.

She smiled at them and stepped aside to allow them to get closer to Joshua. After a few moments, when there was a pause in the conversation that the women were having with him, Sarah excused herself and said she'd be back in a while. Before anything could be said, she walked out of the room and then paced up and down the corridor.

It was hard not knowing if Joshua had meant it when he'd asked her to marry him. There could've been several reasonable explanations for his words. He could've been suffering delirium, he could've had a bump on the head, or he could've meant he was grateful that she found him.

After fifteen minutes, Sarah walked back into the room figuring the children would've had long enough to see him.

"Sarah, where did you go?" Joshua asked.

The women turned and stared at her.

"I just wanted to give everyone time to see you alone. I should go and leave you to rest."

"Stay longer? I've had no chance to speak with you."

"We should probably go, Elizabeth," said Sadie.

"Okay," Elizabeth agreed.

They said their goodbyes, and they left the room.

"Come closer, Sarah," Joshua said.

She stood behind the children and placed a hand on each of their shoulders.

"I'll be home by Christmas," he announced.

"Great!" Benjamin said.

Holly turned around and gave Sarah a big smile.

Sarah smiled back at Holly, and then said, "Only if the doctor says you're well enough."

"I'll be well enough. He thinks I'll be alright in a day or two."

"I hope so."

"We've got the arnica oil, Mrs. Kurtz."

"That's right. That'll help," Joshua said with a smile.

"Why were you in the barn? Nellie had heard you were checking on a barn for someone, but you left in a taxi."

"I had the taxi stop in at a general store to pick something up. I ran into someone there and he was concerned about his barn and whether he should rebuild or knock it down. He was having an issue with his son-in-law about it. It was on the way, so I told him I'd look at it and get back to him."

"So you looked at the barn on your way?"

"Jah. The road got too uneven for the taxi to get close, so it stopped at about the same distance the ambulance had to stop. The beam fell on me and then I yelled out, hoping the driver heard me. I guess when I didn't return, he thought I'd run off without paying the fare, and he left."

"It's a wonder he didn't hear the crash."

"I might have softened that crash somewhat."

Sarah winced at the thought.

"How long were you there, *Dat?*"

"A long time until Mrs. Kurtz found me."

"Were you scared?" Holly asked.

"I prayed and that kept my mind focused. I had to get home to all of you." He looked at his two children and glanced up at Sarah.

A bell sounded, signaling the end of visiting hours.

"We'll come back and see you tomorrow," Sarah said.

Joshua's eyebrows pinched together. *"Nee* don't. It's too much trouble."

Benjamin huffed. "We want to see you, *Dat.*"

"I know, but it's a lot of trouble to get here in the taxi and Mrs. Kurtz has to have someone mind Gretel and get the both of you organized."

"We don't mind," Sarah said.

"See, *Dat?* It's okay with Mrs. Kurtz."

He nodded. "Okay."

The children hugged their father goodbye.

Just as they were walking out of the ward, they ran into the bishop and his wife.

"How is he?" the bishop asked.

"He's doing okay. He might be out in a day or two, but he'll be on crutches."

When the bell sounded again, the bishop said, "I'll go and see him quickly before I'm thrown out."

CHAPTER 22

Let all those that seek thee rejoice and be glad in
thee:
let such as love thy salvation say continually,
The Lord be magnified.
Psalm 40:16

TWO DAYS LATER, it was Christmas Eve and Joshua had been given the all clear to leave the hospital. He had insisted on coming home in a taxi by himself rather than having Sarah coming to get him.

When Joshua's taxi drove up to the house, his two children ran out to him.

Sarah walked out just as the taxi drove away.

He looked up at her. "Hello, Sarah."

"Hello. Do you want to come into my *haus?* I've got a meal ready, or I could bring it into you at your *haus.*"

"I'd like to come into your *haus,* Sarah, *denke.*"

Sarah was surprised. She thought he'd want to get back into his own place.

The children followed him to the couch and then sat by him.

"Look at the tree, *Dat.* Mrs. Kurtz showed us how to make decorations out of paper."

"It looks *wunderbaar.*"

"It kept us busy," Sarah said.

Soon, the children were distracted by

Gretel's cooing. They started showing her some wooden shapes and laughing at her different expressions as she waved her arms and kicked her little legs.

"Would you like *kaffe* or anything?" Sarah asked.

"*Nee,* just come and sit by me."

"I forgot. A letter came for you." She fetched the letter and then handed it to him as she sat down.

"*Denke.*" He ripped it open and unfolded the one sheet of paper. His lips slowly turned upward at the corners as he read. "Well, that's good."

"What's that?"

"My money just came through."

"*Wunderbaar.*"

"Sarah, do you remember what I asked you when I was trapped in that barn?"

"I do, but I'm surprised that *you* remember it."

"I do. And I meant it."

She stared at him. "You did?"

"Come closer."

She leaned closer and then he took her hand, and whispered, "I want to make you my wife. Will you marry me?"

Unable to find words she stared into his eyes.

He continued, "I know we didn't get off well when we first met, and that was entirely my fault. It must have been a shock for you to find us in your *haus*."

Sarah giggled. "It was, and you continued to surprise me."

"I suppose I did and not in a good way. You told me how important Christmas is to you and tomorrow is Christmas day. I want you to have the security to know that we'll all be a family, if that's what you want. I'd marry you tomorrow, but I think the bishop wouldn't be able to marry us that quickly."

She looked down.

"Say something?" he pleaded. "Tell me how you're feeling. I know we probably don't know each other that well, but I feel there's something between us and I'm hoping you feel it too."

"Everything in my life has changed since Joel died. I'm a widow, I'm living in a different place, and now Gretel is here. I do feel the same as what you said, that there's something between us, and it would make me very happy to marry you and we could raise our *kinner* together."

"Really? You mean that?"

She nodded.

"You've made me so happy. When will we tell Benjamin and Holly?"

"What about Christmas morning? It'll be a time for them to always remember. Christmas! I need to start cooking for Christmas and getting everything ready. You and I and the *kinner* have been invited to have the evening meal at Nellie's *haus,* but we'll have two meals here before that."

He laughed. "It doesn't matter what we have. We'll be together. This will be our first Christmas together."

"That's why it has to be perfect."

"It will be, because we'll all be together. I've got plenty of food for Christmas next door. I'll bring it over and we can cook it here."

"I've got plenty too."

"Sarah, I want to explain why I was so awful to you."

"It doesn't matter now. I've got so much to do."

"The children and I will all help. I'm not sick. I'm not even in any pain. I can watch, but I really won't be much use in the kitchen."

"Okay, we'll all make some food ready for tomorrow and you can watch. I'll just give

Gretel her bottle and then we can cook while she's asleep."

Sarah headed to the kitchen to get Gretel her bottle. This was everything she had wanted. She now had a family and her house, this gift from *Onkel* Harold, was full.

CHAPTER 23

Blessed is that man that maketh the Lord his trust, and respecteth not the proud, nor such as turn aside to lies.
Psalm 40:4

IT WAS EARLY in the morning when Joshua and his children came over to her place. Snow was lightly falling, and flakes swept in through the door when they came inside.

After they had greeted one another, Benjamin hurried over and placed some presents under the tree and then he helped his father who was already busy making the fire hotter.

Sarah smiled at Joshua walking in on his crutches and still trying to take over. His attitude had annoyed her at first, but now she knew he wasn't doing it to be demeaning, he was doing things out of genuine goodness, unaware that he might be too forceful in his actions.

Sarah took the opportunity to fetch the surprises that Holly had made for her father and brother and put them under the small tree.

"They'll like them, I'm sure," Sarah whispered to Holly.

Holly smiled and nodded as she stared at the bright paper-wrapped presents.

"Is everyone ready for breakfast?"

"I am," Benjamin said.

"Me too," Holly said, heading to the kitchen.

Joshua pushed on his crutches and straightened himself from his crouched position by the fire.

"Are you feeling okay?" Sarah asked Joshua.

"I've never been better."

Sarah gave a small giggle.

"Gretel's asleep?" Joshua asked.

"Jah, she'll sleep most of the morning. She was up early to eat. Now, I've got pancakes, eggs, bagels…"

"I do have an appetite right now."

"Gut." They headed to the kitchen.

Throughout the breakfast, Sarah was nervous about what Benjamin and Holly would say about her marrying the man they called *'Dat.'* The man who'd raised them and the only parent they'd had for a long time. She glanced over at Joshua, wondering if he'd tell them this morning or later in the day.

Finally, he said, "Benjamin and Holly, I've got something to tell you."

"What is it?"

"Mrs. Kurtz has agreed to marry me."

"Really?" Benjamin looked between the two of them.

Sarah nodded, hoping he'd be okay with it.

"Wait a minute. Does that mean we'll all live in the same *haus?*" Benjamin asked.

"It does."

"Will you be our *Mamm?*" Holly asked.

"I will, and Gretel will be your *schweschder.*"

Holly's eyes opened wide and she clapped her hands together with delight. "I won't be the youngest anymore. Can we call you *Mamm?*" Holly breathlessly pushed some strands of hair away from her face.

Sarah reached over and smoothed her hair. "You can."

"I'm glad you'll be my new *Mamm*," Holly said.

"Can we start calling you *Mamm* now?" Benjamin asked.

Sarah glanced over at Joshua, who said, "You might as well get into the habit of it because she'll be your *Mamm* soon enough."

"When?" Holly asked.

"Four weeks."

Sarah looked up. "That soon?"

"*Jah.* Is that too soon for you?"

She shook her head. "*Nee.*"

"This is the best news I've heard for a long time," Benjamin said.

"Me too," Holly agreed.

"Where will we live? In your new *haus, Dat?*"

"We haven't bought one yet. I'll have to discuss all those kinds of things with your new *mudder.* We might want to stay right here. Who knows?"

"*Jah,* we've got many things to talk about

and we wanted you two to be the first to know." Sarah noticed that Holly looked particularly pleased to be the first to know. "Anyone for more pancakes?"

Benjamin shot up his hand.

"You don't want to get a bellyache, Benjamin. Don't you think you've had enough?"

"Nee, not nearly."

"I'll cook some more. Anyone else?"

"Can I have just one more?" Holly asked in a small voice.

"Of course you can."

After the breakfast was over, Sarah had Holly help her in the kitchen while Joshua and Benjamin sat in the living room watching the snow fall out the window.

"I hope they like what I sewed for them," Holly said.

"They will. I'm certain of it."

Once the kitchen was clean, Sarah walked out of the kitchen holding Holly's hand. "It looks like we have some presents under the tree. Shall we open them?"

"*Jah*," Benjamin called out. "I didn't like to ask, but I was waiting until someone said we should open them."

"Can I give mine out first?" Holly asked.

"Okay," Sarah said as she sat down on the couch.

Holly passed her father and Benjamin their presents and then she passed one to Sarah. "And this is yours, *Mamm*."

"Mine?"

Holly nodded. "It's from the three of us; *Dat* as well."

Sarah looked down at the round parcel and then unwrapped it to see a snow globe. "Oh, it's so beautiful," she said softly.

"We thought it looked like this *haus*," Benjamin said.

Holly said, "Turn it upside down and it looks like it's snowing."

Sarah turned it upside down and watched

as the snowflakes fell. "It's very pretty. I love it. *Denke.*" She turned to look at the others. "Were you waiting for me? You can open Holly's presents now."

Holly stood close by Sarah and watched them open their presents.

Benjamin got his unwrapped first. "Holly, did you sew this?"

"*Jah,* all by myself. Mrs., oh, I mean *Mamm* showed me, and told me how to do it."

"*Denke.* It's really *gut!*"

Holly giggled.

Joshua now had his gift unwrapped.

"Watch and Pray. *Denke,* Holly. It's *wunderbaar.*"

"She sews very well," Sarah said.

"I didn't know how until you showed me," Holly said to Sarah.

"Now you could most likely sew anything you wanted."

Joshua held up the sampler. "I will watch

and pray. I'll find a special place to hang this."

Sarah rose to her feet and handed out her gifts to them. She gave Joshua a coffee grinder, Benjamin a pocket knife, and Holly a sewing kit.

"Holly if you go under that tree, I have something for you and something for Benjamin. They're in the green paper."

"Denke, Dat."

"You haven't opened it yet."

Holly giggled and then opened her present to see that it was another sewing kit.

Holly laughed to see it, and the others joined her.

"We had the same thoughts," Joshua said to Sarah.

"Jah, next time we'll have to discuss these things."

Holly held them both up. "I've got lots of sewing things now. I can sew every day."

"You can." Sarah looked over to see that

Benjamin had just opened his gift and it was a fishing hook and a sinker.

Joshua said, "I couldn't wrap the whole thing. I've got the rest hidden in the barn. It's a new fishing rod."

"Wow! *Denke, Dat.*"

Gretel's cries were heard from the bedroom upstairs.

"I'll get her a bottle and she can join us."

Soon, Gretel was nestled in Sarah's arms drinking her bottle.

"*Dat,* can we play some games?"

"*Jah,* that would be a *gut* idea. Do you have any here, Sarah?"

"*Nee,* I don't. I haven't had any since I was a child and it'll be a while before Gretel is ready for games."

"Benjamin, go back to the *haus* and bring some back."

Benjamin disappeared and came back a few minutes later with an armful of games. The children were settled down with the games while Sarah and Joshua stared at one another from across the couch.

"You're too far away. It's easier for you to move than me with these crutches."

Sarah stood up with Gretel in her arms and sat next to him.

"I was miserable until you arrived here, Sarah. That's why I was horrible to you because inside I was wretched. You've changed me, Sarah Kurtz."

She gave a little giggle. "*Gott* listened to my prayers and He knows how I feel about Christmas and *familye*. I've got the *familye* that I've always wanted and we're all here together on Christmas day." Sarah stared into Joshua's green eyes, knowing that he'd always look after her and Gretel just as he'd taken on the role of father to Holly and Benjamin.

God had taken away Sarah's first love, Joel, for reasons of His own and she'd had no choice in that. After Joel's death, Sarah prayed that she'd never be alone and now she had more than another husband—she had a ready-made family.

Let all those that seek thee rejoice and be glad in thee: let such as love thy salvation say continually,
The Lord be magnified.
Psalm 40:16

Thank you for reading Amish Widow's Christmas.

www.SamanthaPriceAuthor.com

THE NEXT BOOK IN THE SERIES

Book 13
Amish Widow's New Hope.

Isla and her boyfriend planned to marry and then return to their Amish community.

A tragic accident caused Isla to continue their plans alone.

When Isla learns she's pregnant, her joy is overshadowed by worry that she won't find forgiveness in her Amish family.

Isla does her best to create a new life while struggling with guilt and loss.

Will Isla let go of the past so she can embrace what God has designed for her future?

EXPECTANT AMISH WIDOWS

Book 7 A Pregnant Widow's Amish Vacation

Book 8 The Amish Firefighter's Widow

Book 9 Amish Widow's Secret

Book 10 The Middle-Aged Amish Widow

Book 11 Amish Widow's Escape

Book 12 Amish Widow's Christmas

Book 13 Amish Widow's New Hope

Book 14 Amish Widow's Story

Book 15 Amish Widow's Decision

Book 16 Amish Widow's Trust

Book 17 The Amish Potato Farmer's Widow

Book 18 Amish Widow's Tears

Book 19 Amish Widow's Heart

ALL SAMANTHA PRICE'S BOOK SERIES

Amish Maids Trilogy

Amish Love Blooms

Amish Misfits

The Amish Bonnet Sisters

Amish Women of Pleasant Valley

Ettie Smith Amish Mysteries

Amish Secret Widows' Society

Expectant Amish Widows

Seven Amish Bachelors

Amish Foster Girls

Amish Brides

Amish Romance Secrets

Amish Twin Hearts

Amish Wedding Season

Amish Baby Collection

Gretel Koch Jewel Thief

Made in United States
Orlando, FL
28 June 2023

34607416R00157